Cuckolded by A Slutty Stripper

A Femdom Cuckolding Love Story

Omnibus Edition

Jenna Masters

2022

Contents

The base of the music echoed through the floor of the strip-club, up through Andrea's platform stripper heels, up her slim, perfectly tan legs, and up her spine. She continued the rhythm of the beat, through her neck, as she bobbed her head, blonde hair spilling over the young stud's lap. She slurped loudly, the fat cock stretching her lips and filling her throat with blissful heat and powerful throbbing.

"That's it," the guy moaned as her glossy red lips slid up and down his pole. "Earn that sixty-bucks."

Andrea didn't care about the extra sixty bucks, but she'd take it. The truth was, when a guy with a cock as big and beautiful as this got her into the VIP room, she just couldn't help herself. She'd already fingered herself to completion, and now she just needed to finish him off. She bobbed her head faster and faster, knowing he was close, feeling the pressure building in his thick, powerful meat.

"Yes," he moaned. "Oh, fuck yes." Then he began to explode, filling her hungry mouth with thick, hot, delicious jizz. She gulped him down, slowing her pace, carefully milking the last drops of his seed until the twitching stopped and he began to soften. She slipped him out of her mouth, got her money off the table, and pulled her plaid tube-top back over her small, perky breasts.

"Thanks, Baby," she said, standing up. "Be sure and look for me next time you stop by."

He gave her ass an affectionate spank, his big hand slapping the smooth flesh of her small, round ass through the thin fabric of her pleated plaid skirt. "You know it, slut," he said.

Andrea giggled, waved, and slipped out of the VIP room, counting the twenties that she had earned. The guy was still on the couch, blissfully relaxed, his balls thoroughly drained. Of course, Andrea didn't blow every guy that took her to the VIP room. But when she had felt that virile, young jock's magnificent, and powerful erection pressing against her ass as she ground back against him, she couldn't wait to have it in her mouth.

She thought of the college boy as young, even though she herself was barely over twenty-three. But her four years as a stripper had provided her with many, many experiences and brought her into contact with many diverse types of guys. The ones that went for the slinky blonde girl's thin, tanned body were usually the older, daddy types. Those types of men loved her slender frame, and her small, perky breasts. They were the reason she wore slutty schoolgirl uniforms most nights. The one she wore now was a tiny, pleated skirt that barely covered her panties and showed off the length of her thin, brown legs, and a tight little pleated top that constantly threatened to slip down and reveal her perky round breasts. She finished the outfit with towering black platform stripper heels.

Andrea finished counting her cash and pushed it back in her clutch-purse. She still needed more money tonight, but her heart wasn't in it. She had gotten all hot and bothered as she slurped and sucked that gorgeous cock, one of her fingers pressing down her panties and rubbing her clit. She had cum hard and followed it up by swallowing down that warm and delicious load of salty sperm, and now she felt drained. She just wanted to go home and curl up with someone. Of course, there was no one waiting at home to curl up with. She straightened out her pleated skirt and checked her reflection in one of the thousands of mirrors in the strip club. Someday, after she had made all the money she could, and gotten hammered by all the hot "bad-boy" types she craved, then she could find a nice, sweet guy to settle down with. Till then, she had work to do. She pulled out her lip-gloss and applied a fresh, glistening layer.

Andrea turned and scanned the crowd for new arrivals and her eyes immediately set on a slim young man towards the back corner. He sat alone at a table in the darkest edge of the club, as if embarrassed to be there. He wore simple, clean clothes and his eyes darted around, one minute staring, the next moment turning away when someone noticed his attention.

Not my usual type, Andrea thought. *But good for a few bucks.*

She slithered up to his table and sat down on his lap without invitation. "Hi," she purred. "Feeling lonely?"

She was surprised to feel his nervous pulse, thundering through his thin frame. She hadn't felt this kind of nervous, struggling intensity in a boy since high school. He still struggled to answer the first question when she asked him another. "Come here often?"

"First time," he said. His voice was sweet, even as it broke with nervous insecurity.

Back in school, when she had let nervous, struggling guys carry her books and follow her around like puppies, she had always got a thrilling sense of power from their desperation. But she had given all that up when the hot, older boys started noticing her. Now, when she encountered the nervous ones, she would normally sell them a few dances and move on. But there was something sweet about this one. He smelled nice, his breath minty, a hint of vanilla to his soft, clean skin. She wiggled closer to his comfortable frame. "Buy me a drink?" she offered.

"Okay," he said.

She gave another little wiggle, rubbing her ass in his lap as a reward, and was surprised to feel him instantly go hard. His erection was small and thin but powerfully swollen, throbbing desperately beneath her slim brown thigh. She flagged the waitress and ordered a triple shot screwdriver.

"What's your name?" she asked the sweet voiced, nice smelling little man after the waitress had left. She slithered off his lap and onto the chair next to him so she could see his face, but extended one long, slim leg, resting the platform of one of her slutty heels on his lap possessively.

He squirmed as his little bulge rubbed against the edge of her heel. "I... my name's Tim."

"Kim?" she pretended to mishear with a devious thrill. Something about this nervous man just brought out the bitch in her.

He swallowed and blushed. "Tim," he said again, seeming terrified to correct her.

"It's a pleasure to meet you Kim," she said. "It's a very unusual name for a guy, but I like it. It fits you." She leaned forward and held out her hand for him. He took it and shook it nervously, not correcting her again.

Andrea laughed. She wasn't sure what the hell she was doing. This was no way to work a customer. She should be feeding his ego and stroking his desperate and pathetic fantasies of ever getting a girl like her, but instead she found herself intoxicated with power, watching him squirm.

Her drink came and she began to inhale it, as Tim kept nursing his beer. His glances kept passing over her slender body whenever she turned to look at one of the dancers, but then dropped to his lap when she turned back. Andrea watched this happen for the third time then gave her foot a little shake, rubbing it somewhat roughly against his still straining little bulge.

"Are you some kind of foot perv, Kim?"

He looked back up at her face, shocked. "Wha… what?" he asked.

Andrea laughed. "You just keep staring at my feet. It's okay. I don't care if you're a foot perv. I meet lots of freaks in here."

"No, I'm not looking at your feet, I just…"

She moved her foot in his lap, turning it gently now, stroking him slightly with her dirty heel. "It's okay. Just admit you're a foot perv. I'm not judging you. You don't have to be ashamed, Kim."

"Tim," he squeaked.

"Kim," she purred, watching him squirm as she rubbed him through his slacks with her slutty stripper heel. "As a foot perv, how would you rate my feet? Are they the kind of feet you'd just love to kiss?"

He looked down at her slender foot, the slutty, strappy stripper-heel turning in his lap. "Their beautiful," he admitted.

Andrea laughed again. "Oh my god, I was just teasing you. But you really are a foot perv."

She wasn't sure why she was tormenting this poor guy, exploiting his eager, needy desperation, but she felt strangely aroused. She was more aroused now, turning her heel in this needy guy's lap, then she had even been as she fingered herself to completion, sucking a hot stud's gorgeous cock just a few minutes before. The slim, needy boy, who must be twenty-one to get in this place, but didn't look a day over nineteen, seemed not only willing to take her abuse, but he seemed to welcome it with a sense of thrilling surrender.

As the boy tried to deny his foot fetish, Andrea slipped her foot out of her platform heel and raised her long, slender leg. The boy stared down that long leg, glowing in the clubs red-filtered lights, down to the flesh of her inner thigh, and the red lace of her skimpy panties showing through the gap in her tiny skirt.

"Kiss it," she said. "Kiss my foot. It's okay."

He stared at her foot, nervous and hesitating.

"It's okay," she said. "You have my permission to be a dirty little foot perv, Kim. Kiss it."

He was actually blushing as he lowered his face, and with an almost reverent softness, kissed her instep.

Andrea purred and laughed, turning up her dainty panted toes and pressing them to his lips. She pushed her toes gently into his mouth, and he sucked them gently and nervously.

He grew more animated and seemed more comfortable now that he was being told what to do. Still, she wasn't here to humiliate needy, inexperienced guys, as much as she found herself enjoying it. She was here to make money.

"How much cash do you have with you right now?" she suddenly asked. She plucked her toes from his mouth and brought her foot back down to his lap with an indifferent, jarring concussion.

Tim winced. "Four hundred," he answered.

She slipped her foot back into her towering heel and stood up. She held out her hand for him, amazed how easy the adorable, nervous boy was to control. "Come on, Kim. We're going to the VIP room." He followed her obediently, not even asking the fees as she led him away from his table to a separate, curtained off area.

She turned to him, once inside, pressed herself against him and guided him with the soft curves of her slender body, pushing him to sitting on a small red sofa. She hovered over him, feeling his pulse pounding through his body, his eyes darting around, not sure where to look.

She slipped off her top and his eyes went to her small, firm breasts. He swallowed hard, staring at her hard, pink nipples and perky brown breasts. "Do you like my tits?" she asked.

"Yes," he whimpered breathlessly, desperately, his hands at his sides and his erection throbbing beneath her.

She arched her back and brought her hard, pink nipples a fraction of an inch from his lips. She could feel his heavy, intensified breathing, passing over the tender flesh of her sensitive breasts. She expected him to bury his face in her tits, but he sat, eyes wide and hungry, erection throbbing, hands at sides.

"Good boy," she purred.

She slipped off his lap and wiggled out of her little schoolgirl skirt. She threw it over his head, making him wear it like a scarf or a loose, perfume scented collar. She turned away from him and slithered back onto his lap.

He moaned in delicious, desperate pleasure as her soft ass pressed against his hard erection through the fabric of his slacks. She purred, grinding her small, round ass into his lap.

"Can I touch you," he asked softly, a little break of desperation in his voice.

Of course, most guys didn't ask. Most guys would have their hands all over her by now. She supposed there were some girls here that didn't like being groped by the men in the club, hell, a lot of the girls here were actually lesbians, but Andrea loved it. She loved making strange men hard as their big hands ran across her smooth, tanned skin. She always made great tips, not just because she let guys go farther with her than most girls, but because she genuinely loved it. She loved it so much she was constantly losing control, regularly letting herself get fingerbanged in the back corner for twenty bucks a song or sucking some guy off just to feel that hard, pulsating meat between her lips.

But this man was so sweet and well behaved, his hands by his sides, that small but rock-hard erection throbbing in his pants. He was like an obedient little puppy, desperate to be pet. "No," she told him in a sweet, purring voice. "Be a good boy. Follow the rules. No touching." She continued to rub her small, curved ass back into his lap, feeling his little hardon throb beneath his slacks, curious just how well behaved this sweet boy would be.

She positioned her ass and positioned his bulge. Soon, his fabric covered hardon was squeezed between her little brown ass-cheeks, pressing against her thong as she rubbed up and down the short distance of his erection. "So, what kind of stuff do you like?" she purred. "When your fucking, I mean. What do you like to do to a girl, or have a girl do to you?"

His voice was breaking, uncomfortable, his face red, even as his little dick pulsated against the smooth flesh of her soft little ass. "Please let me touch you," he begged.

"I said, follow the rules," she warned him in a lustrous, purring voice. "Don't make me call one of the bouncers in here." The thought of one of the massive bouncers towering over this sweet little man made her tingle, as she continued grinding her little ass against his small hardon. "Now answer my question."

"I don't know," he said. "I'm a virgin."

Andrea laughed. "Awe…" she said, with teasing, flirty sympathy. "Why is that? Is it because of your little dick? Are you afraid girls will make fun of it?"

He swallowed hard, not speaking, his body hot with shame even as his cock throbbed beneath her. "Is it… Is it really that…"?

Andrea laughed again. Why was she getting so wet? "I'm just teasing you," she said. He was small though, or possibly closer to average, but when was the last time she had settled for average? "Besides, size isn't everything." Then, purring with more fake sympathy she added, "Not every guy can have a big, amazing cock. Lots of girls are happy to settle for a nice, cute, little dick like yours." She stroked him faster, pressing her curves against his nervous body. He was quiet, eyes closed, perhaps at the edge of tears, but his dick was still throbbing between her smooth brown cheeks. Why was it turning her on so much to be such a bitch, and why was he still so turned on?

She threw her head back and caressed him with her silky hair as she continued to grind up and down his lap. She arched her back and rubbed the side of her face against his cheek, inhaling the scent of her own perfume rising from the skirt around his neck. "Girls shouldn't have to pretend a guy like you is a big, strong man, with a big, powerful cock and guys like you shouldn't need to pretend either. You should be free to be the sweet, agreeable little pet you were meant to be." His dick twitched beneath her.

Andrea was so fucking wet. She didn't know what it was about this skinny, nervous guy that was turning her on so much. It had started out as just a game. She had wanted to see how far she could go, when he would finally stand up and say enough, when he would finally put up a fight, but that point had come and gone, without a whisper. Now, she felt victorious and found herself getting hotter. She had become used to pretending all the guys in here were studs, but talking to a man like this, treating a man like this and having him accept it and wait desperately for more, was surprisingly thrilling. And this adorable little virgin, so needy and well-behaved, so cute and well-groomed… she found herself really drawn to him.

"I'm sorry," he whimpered softly.

"For what? For your little dick?" She laughed again, continuing to stroke him with her lithe little body. "You don't have to apologize. You should be proud of the cute little thing. You're perfect, from your cute face to your sweet manners to your tiny, desperate little dicklette." She arched her back even more, small tits pointing at the ceiling, then turned her face and kissed his cheek.

"Thank you," he whimpered, his voice raising in pitch as his desperate excitement grew. "Thank you."

Andrea recognized his quickened breath and began grinding harder and faster against him. She felt his chest moving in quick, frantic breaths as her body worked. She extended her tongue and pressed it into his ear. No sooner had the wet tip of her tongue touched his ear, and her glossy red lips pressed to his earlobe, then he let out a whimper. His dick began to twitch and shoot hot wads of salty spunk into his slacks. She could feel the sticky heat against her ass as she continued to grind him to completion, tongue wiggling in his ear.

"Oh fuck," he whimpered, as his body convulsed with the last pulses of orgasm.

She purred into his ear, "That was an easy four hundred bucks."

She slipped off his lap and he instantly began to fumble for his wallet. He pulled out the bills and handed them over.

She looked at him there. He was attractive in a safe, unthreatening way and he looked adorable and needy with his slacks stained with cum, and her pleated skirt around his neck like a marking of ownership. "I don't usually do anything like this," she lied. "Getting guys off in the VIP room. I'm not that type of girl. I'm actually a very normal girl." She slipped her skirt over his head and began to step back into it.

"I wish…" he hesitated nervously. "I wish, I wish I could get to know you. Like, outside of here."

She smiled at his sweet, innocent neediness. He smiled back, gazing into her eyes instead of staring at her naked breasts. She leaned in and gave him a kiss on the lips, her tongue, still salty with the taste of her last trip to the VIP room, pressed into his mouth. He kissed her back with eager inexperience, and when she finally pulled her lips away from his, he gazed at her with utter love and complete devotion.

He sat in silence as she slithered into her top, then tucked the money into her panties. She bent over and reached down to the little coffee table. She wiggled her small, round ass side to side, letting him get a good, long look as she wrote her number on a napkin. "Call me tomorrow. You can take me someplace nice." She stood up and gave him a sideways glance as she handed him her number. Normally, she would never consider meeting a guy from the club. But she felt weirdly fond and possessive of her well-behaved little pet. "Be on your best behavior, though. You're sweet, and I can't have you acting like some regular jerk all the sudden."

"I promise," he said.

"Good boy," she purred again, before she bent over and kissed his cheek once more. She then straightened, turned, and strolled away, feeling his eyes moving up and down her slim, mostly naked body.

Andrea was turned on again, and within an hour she was blowing another guy in the VIP room and had forgotten all about her new little pet.

Filthy Fun Before Their First Date

Andrea almost didn't answer the phone. She didn't recognize the caller ID and she'd forgotten all about giving her number to Tim. Her lover had wandered onto the patio of the hotel room to smoke a cigarette. She turned over in bed, her small brown tits sticky with cum. "Hello," she answered.

"Andrea?"

The nervous male voice on the other side was met with silence and so it spoke again.

"It's me, Tim."

More silence.

"You gave me your number at the club. Um... you kept calling me Kim..."

Andrea involuntarily smiled as she remembered the sweet, nervous little man. What had possessed her to give him her number? "Hi there, Sweetie," she purred.

"Hi," she could almost hear him blushing. "I was hoping... did you still want to get together for a... for a date?"

There had to be some reason she had given the boy her number. He definitely was not her type. Her type was older, meaner, and much, much bigger. Still, she couldn't think about nervous little Timmy without smiling and feeling a strange warmness in her tummy. At least she could get a nice meal out of it. "Of course, Sweetie. You know Alexander's on Fourth Street. Meet me there at seven?"

"Yes," he agreed quickly, not flinching at the high-priced location.

"Good boy," she said. "See you then." She hung up the phone and realized at some point in her talk, her lover had come back inside. She laughed, realizing he was still naked, and had stood out on the balcony like that, his big limp dick dangling between his thighs, glistening with her vaginal juices.

The handsome, still muscular early forties man looked her over again, as if reappraising her tight, brown twenty-three-year-old body. "Who was that?" he asked.

"No one, Daddy," she purred. "Just some loser who's going to buy me dinner."

The man laughed, confident and at ease. Andrea didn't think Tim was a loser exactly, but she was sure this man would have, and besides, men like this loved hearing smaller, weaker men degraded by the hot girls they fucked. The man pulled the covers down, revealing the rest of Andrea's long, slinky body. He looked her up and down, from her perky young tits to her slim, shaved cunt. "You said seven," he pointed out. "What makes you think I'll be done with you by then?"

Andrea stretched out, arching her body, and showing off her lithe little figure. "Do your worst, Daddy. He can wait."

The handsome older man moved onto the bed, moving on his knees. Andrea rose to meet him on her knees as well, moving as if about to kiss him, then dropping to her elbows at the last minute, lowering her face to his still limp cock. She lifted his big, serpentine meat and pressed it to her lips, giving it a soft kiss before slipping it between her lips. He moaned, looking down at her little round ass and shimmering blonde hair as she began to suck him hard. As his dick grew and began to throb in her mouth, she slid her lips all the way to the base, then back up to the tip. She slipped her lips from the thick, delicious meat, a line of drool connecting her little pink tongue to the throbbing mushroom head. He was fully, impressively hard now. The man was both a shower and a grower, and his dick looked beautiful, light shimmering in her drool as it dribbled down the thick, rippled surface.

She smiled tauntingly at the older man. "When's the last time your wife deepthroated this big, beautiful cock?" she asked.

She idly traced the bulging veins of this massive shaft with her fingertips, tracing the tiny bubbles of her saliva across his rippled tool.

He ignored the question and placed one massive hand on her small skull, gently but unwaveringly directing her mouth back onto his meat. Andrea did not resist, loving the feeling of his quiet, commanding power. He drove himself forward between her lips, easing his powerful cock steadily forward. She slurped wetly as she moved her head forward to meet him, driving his bulging prick down her narrow throat with a hint of a gag, followed by a long, throaty moan.

"Yes," he moaned. "That's it. Good girl."

She drew her lips back, slurping up her own saliva with her skilled little mouth, then slid her lips forward again. She began to bob her head, making lurid gulping and gagging sounds as her lips moved back and forth along the ridges of his massive, swollen meat. She purred, vibrations caressing his rod as she continued driving him in and out of her wet esophagus.

"Yes," her lover moaned. "Oh, fuck yes. That's my girl. That's my slutty little stripper girl."

Andrea slurped faster. She loved it when he talked dirty. She loved being his slutty little stripper girl. She longed to someday be someone's pure, and beautiful love, but for now, she loved being dirty trash for this powerful, older man. She gulped and slobbered as he moaned. Her pace grew faster and the suction of her seasoned mouth more intense. She listened to the man's clues; the way his body shivered and swayed, the sound of his voice, the depth of his breathing, and she used those clues to adjust her pressure and speed, gulping him down with ever increasing hunger.

Her naked ass wiggled side to side as she slurped up and down his cock. Soft blonde hair tickled her slender back, and his muscular thighs.

His hand on her skull went from gentle to insistent, fingers twisting in her hair. "That's my slut," he groaned. "That's my whore. Make Daddy cum before you go out on your date with your lovesick little loser."

Andrea doubted her loser was lovesick yet, but he did seem very sweet. The thought of him getting ready for their date right now, nervous and needy, as she slobbered on another man's cock, filled her with a surprising thrill.

She savored the sensation of hot cock bulging in her throat. She caressed the swollen contours and veins with her tongue, rested her lips on the thick, throbbing shaft. Her pussy tingled and began to flood, but she was still satisfied from the earlier fucking. Right now, she only wanted to serve. She wanted to worship this magnificent cock until it exploded for her.

Andrea gazed up at the older man, eyes pleading for his thick, powerful seed.

"Yes," he groaned. "Oh, fuck yes. That's my girl. That's my hungry little slut. Fuck yes."

She gazed up at the older man, her eyes full of submissive hunger as she slurped up and down the length of his pole. Her whole body rocking; her little ass swaying side to side as she gobbled up his cock. She knew her tiny face and narrow throat looked shocking, swallowing his massive meat, and she savored the look in his eyes as she slurped him in and out of her esophagus with a soft, subtle gagging sound.

"Fuck," he moaned, getting closer, his big hand on the crown of her small skull. "Oh fuck. My dirty little stripper girl. My filthy little stripper slut."

Slobber ran down his pole and dripped down his hairy balls. She wanted to lick up the glistening drool, but she knew he was close. She focused on jamming him in and out of her throat with a steady rhythm as one of her hands reached up, fingers teasing the saliva drenched hairs of his balls.

His breathing increased, his abs and the muscles of his thighs flexed, and he groaned with shuddering ecstasy.

Andrea felt a hot wad of jizz blast into her throat as the man above her shook and moaned with orgasm. Andrea gulped the wad down as she pulled the tip from her throat. His sperm continued to explode into her mouth, thick and salty. She grasped his shaft and pulled his fat tip across the surface of her tongue towards her lips. She swallowed another musky mouthful of testosterone rich cream before she pulled him fully from her mouth, letting his dick explode above her face. She stroked his twitching erection above her as he continued to rain spunk down on her pretty face.

She gazed up at the older man, her occasional lover, as he spewed hot, sticky seed all over her face. Her lips stretched wide, tongue extended, she caught another wad of jizz, letting it drip from her tongue and drop into her mouth, as other wads of cum dripped down the skin of her face.

When the eruption finally ended, leaving her youthful face streaked with cum and her mouth pooled with potent seed, she licked her lips, smearing them with cum, then swallowed her warm mouthful.

The man moaned with release, then sighed with satisfaction. He looked down at her, meeting her gaze with a strong, confident smile. He pat her head like she was a pet and said, "Be sure and give your new boyfriend a nice big kiss with that filthy little mouth."

She was about to point out that Tim wasn't her boyfriend, but Thomas had already turned away and started getting dressed. She wiped the cum off her face with the edge of a hotel sheet and began dressing as well. She slipped her feet into her heels and slithered into her little black dress. The flimsy little dress would have looked casual and innocent, if it wasn't so short that it barely covered the cleft of her tight, round ass.

Twenty minutes later Andrea was sitting in the back of a cab, pulling up to front of a very expensive restaurant.

"That will be forty-seven eighty-two," the cab driver said as the car came to a stop in front of the building.

Andrea suddenly realized she forgot to get cab-fare from Mark, and she didn't have her wallet. "Shit," she said. "I don't have it." She leaned forward, smiling her dirtiest smile, and framing the cleavage of her small, perky breasts with her slender arms. "Maybe you can let me get up front and I can pay you another way?"

The driver sighed as if he'd heard this said before. He looked in his rearview mirror, adjusting it down then up again. "Yeah," he said, his tone changed, suddenly excited as if it was the first time he'd really looked at her. He reached up and unlocked the passenger side door. "Come on up, we'll talk it over."

"You can talk if you like," she said as she slipped out the back door. "I'm going to have my mouth full."

As she stepped out of the car, she saw Tim through the front glass of the restaurant, seated in the waiting area. He noticed her and rose to his feet, giving her an excited wave. Andrea waved back, then held up one finger to indicate he should wait a minute. She slid into the seat and leaned over, her hand going to the driver's zipper. "Can you turn the headlights back on?" she asked. "I don't want my date to see what I'm doing in here."

The driver laughed as he turned on the headlights. "You're quite a catch," he said.

"He's just a date," Andrea pointed out as she leaned over the middle-aged cabdriver's lap. "He's not my boyfriend or anything." She unzipped him, rubbing her hair and face across his beer belly. Andrea arched her back, knees on the seat, ass high. She wiggled her body so her dress worked down, giving the cabdriver a nice view of her tanned, curving ass and the little pink thong. She had to make this quick. She loved savoring a nice cock, and she could tell from the bulge in the cabdriver's slacks, that he had a very nice cock. But this was strictly business, and she had places to be. Still, as rushed as she was, she couldn't resist pointing out, "If he was my boyfriend or something, I would be a good girl."

The man laughed doubtfully as he put a hand on her ass, but he said, "You seem like a very good girl to me."

Her hand slid into his underwear. Her fingers clasped around his thick, throbbing erection, feeling his powerful pulse thumping hotly in the soft, cool skin of her hand. She tingled all over as she pulled his impressive tool out. She studied it for a moment, forgetting herself as she inhaled his powerful, masculine scent. "You have a pretty big cock. Have you ever been deep-throated before?"

The man shivered with expectation, his big hand squeezing her ass-cheek, finger teasing her crack. "No," he said. "My ex…"

His words turned into a moan as she bowed her head down and with one, fluid gulp, drove him down her throat. She began to bob her head up and down, gurgling luridly as she worked him in and out of her tight esophagus.

"Oh fuck," he moaned, his hand squeezing tighter on her little, round ass. "Oh, fuck yes."

She slurped and drooled, her head bobbing up and down steadily, her mind focused back on her mission. She pumped him with her lips and throat, already driving with a relentless pace. She wiggled her ass against his hand, loving his powerful grip and his fingertips so close to her warm cunt and tight, little asshole. She drove him through her throat a few more times, then spit him back up. She wrapped her hand around his thick tool and began to jerk him fiercely. His dick was glistening in the bluish dashboard lights, her saliva seeming to glow. She licked up some of that saliva and purred, "Go ahead. It's okay. Finger me. Finger my asshole while I suck your big, hard cock."

She took him back in her mouth, stroking him now with her lips, her hand, and her throat.

His fingers pushed her thong aside and she felt one digit teasing her tight, puckered hole.

"Mmmmm," she moaned on his dick, as her entire torso rose and fell in thrashing, frantic waves, fingers and lips locked to his shaft.

He drove his finger into her, moaning with pleasure. He began to drive that finger back and forth in her tight, little asshole as she slurped and sucked loudly on his big, throbbing cock. She could feel his breathing increasing, his pulse thundering through his rod.

She slipped her lips off him again and whimpered. "Feed me mister. Finger my tight little asshole while you feed me your hot, delicious cum."

She was going to say more, to fill his ears with filthy images to get him off, but he was already there, his finger knuckle deep in her rectum, his body beginning to spasm. She slipped her lips back over his rod just in time to catch the first, hot spray of delicious jizz. She gulped it down, for the second time that night, tasting the delicious explosion of hot, musky sperm. Her head bobbing and her fist pumping, she slurped and swallowed. She gulped down jet after jet of salty, warm ecstasy, as the man convulsed beneath her, his finger planted deep in her asshole.

Finally, the cab-driver's body relaxed. His big dick was still twitching in her mouth, but he was completely dry. She spit him out of her mouth, wiggled off his finger and began fixing her thong and dress. She was about to slip out of the cab when he stopped her.

"Wait," he said, frantically retrieving a business card from his console and pressing it towards her. "Next time you need a ride..."

She dropped the card in her little purse, blew the cabdriver a kiss and slipped out of the car. She didn't have the heart to tell the cabbie it wasn't ever going to happen again. She wasn't a whore, and if she ever decided to become one, her blowjobs were worth a lot more than cab-fare. He had just been in the right place at the right time.

Andrea savored the taste of the cabdriver's cum as she walked across the parking lot, Tim waving to her with child-like enthusiasm from the window of the restaurant. He had been seated in the time she'd spent blowing the cabdriver. She stepped in, waved off the hostess and walked, towards the table. She could see Tim's eyes, focused on her with unrestrained adoration as she approached. He looked as if he'd never seen a girl before, and she loved the way the intensity of his interest made her feel. She swayed as she walked, cat-walking slow and watching him. She felt like a predatory animal, stalking her prey as she finally reached the table. "Hi," she purred.

He stood up, his voice breaking slightly. "You… you look…. You're beautiful."

She felt drunk with the intensity of his awe-struck gaze, and she was unable to resist the urge to press against him, grab his slim sides and kiss him savagely on the lips. He melted against her, wiry and weak, dizzy with surprise as she slipped her tongue, still salty with a stranger's cum, into his eager mouth. She kissed him for a moment then stepped back, smiling and gauging his reaction.

Tim was red with arousal and embarrassment, that little erection of his poking his slacks, but he showed no sign of understanding or suspicion. Andrea giggled at his reaction. "Sit down," she spoke in a light, but commanding tone. "Order us some appetizers."

He sat down immediately and waved for the waiter. She marveled at her strange reaction to this man, and the thrill she got from his eager obedience, as she slithered onto the chair across from him.

Through dinner they made small-talk, and she found herself enjoying his attention, his agreeable nature, and his surprising humor. Could she be with a man like this? He was, in so many ways, what she had always imagined when she thought of settling down someday with a "nice" guy. But, of course, the nice guy she had imagined was also six foot tall, handsome, and powerfully endowed. Tim had a nice-looking face, but was small, slim and... well... considerably less blessed than most guys.

Still, did those things matter? So what if he didn't look like prince charming? And as for his not having a big dick; it was all relative, she'd been told. If she was with only him, and stopped getting fucked by big, hard cocks, she would adapt, and become used to his small size. It was only in the comparison where size mattered. Faithful girls could get off just as hard whatever size their man, or so she'd been told.

"Do you want dessert?" Tim asked suddenly and her attention came back to him.

"No thanks," she said. "In fact, I should probably go. Could you drive me home?"

He lit up and quickly paid the bill. On the ride back home, he listened to her talk and made sweet, supportive comments. He pulled in front of her house, got out and walked her to her door. She thought about inviting him inside, but remembered this was a nice guy, and you weren't supposed to fuck nice guys on the first date. "I had a nice time," she told him.

"Me too," he said. "Maybe we can do it again?"

She took his face in her hands, leaned in, and kissed him, pressing her tongue between his lips for just a moment before leaning back out of his space. "I work tomorrow," she said. "But you can pick me up after my shift."

"Okay," he said.

"Be waiting for me in the parking lot around midnight. I'll text you."

"Okay," he said eagerly. "I'll be there."

"Good boy," she purred, giving him a flirty smile, then turned and slipped off into her house, leaving him staring at her slinky body as she left.

A Taste of Things to Come

Andrea still had a wild, giddy feeling from her first date with Tim last night. Something about Tim's eager attention and sweet doting nature, made her feel warm and special in a surprising and exciting way. She felt more confident and desirable than she had in a long time, and it was helping her work. Something about the glow of her new-found joy made her even more popular, as she gave lap-dance after lap-dance; eager men shoving bills into her thong. Early in the night she had already made what she normally made in a full shift of grinding and gyrating against horny, drunken men, and she'd spent the rest of her shift sitting at the bar and relaxing. She had perhaps been relaxing a little too much, as now she felt a little drunk herself. And more than a little horny.

She remembered that she had made a date with Tim again tonight. The little guy might even get lucky this time. She ordered another drink and started fumbling with her clutch, looking for her phone to send Tim a text.

She stopped looking when she felt someone's eyes on her. She looked behind her. It was Thomas, one of her regulars. By regulars, of course she meant he would pay her for a few dances, and she'd end up sucking him off in VIP because he had such a big, amazing cock and toned, muscular body. He stood over six foot tall, towering over her as he approached with his cocky, confident smile.

He put his hand, big and warm and the small of her back, making her shudder. He waved to the bartender. "I'll take a beer and Andy will have a double of whatever she's drinking."

Andrea smiled, swallowed the excess saliva that formed in her mouth at the thought of this man's delicious cock, and said, "I was actually about to go."

"No," he said with a calm, easy smile. "I just got here, girl. Let's have a few drinks." He got the bartender's attention and flashed two fingers, then pointed at Andrea, doubling her order. The slinky Asian bartender smiled knowingly as she brought the beer, and two double screwdrivers and laid them on the bar. Thomas paid for the drinks with a generous tip and a flirty smile, then turned to Andrea and put an arm around her, hand resting commandingly on one of her curving hips. She became aware of how much of her skin was exposed, his strong, calloused fingers caressing her bare midriff between the tiny mini-skirt and the small lace top she wore over her bright red bra.

"I'm meeting someone," she said. Downing one of the screwdrivers in a single swig to emphasize that she wasn't going to stay.

"Your boyfriend?" he asked.

"Just a date," she said, taking a long swig of her second screwdriver.

"Wont he wait?" Thomas said. "If he deserves you, I think he'd be happy to wait." He gestured for the bartender to bring her two more drinks.

Andrea knew that sweet little Tim would wait if she asked him to. He would do anything she asked him to. The strange enthusiasm she got from the idea of seeing Tim washed over her. She felt warm and wet. The thumping base of the sound system reverberated through the barstool, and she could feel it in her cunt. She thought about Thomas's cock, throbbing and pulsating in her mouth. She finished her drink just as the bartender brought her two more, giving her an encouraging wink.

"I suppose a few more couldn't hurt," Andrea said.

"That a girl," Thomas said, squeezing her hip with his big hand.

By the time she finished the two drinks she had gone from buzzed and a little horny, to drunk and fully primed. Thomas's big hand caressed up and down her side making her shiver with need. The closeness of his body, softness of his touch and memory of his amazing cock were making her crazy now.

"I really have to go soon," she said. "But maybe you want a dance first?"

He smiled, reached in his pocket and dropped two fifties on the table. "Let's just go straight to the VIP room," he said.

She downed the rest of her drink, slid the bills into her panties, then stood got up. She took a step, tottering on her massive heels, realizing suddenly how drunk she was. Thomas put his arm around her again, supported her, his deep voice tingling down her spine as he spoke into her ear. "It's okay. I've got you girl."

She giggled and thanked him, purring against him as he helped her walk to the private room. He brought her into the private room, and he half helped, half pushed her onto the couch.

She looked up at him, standing over her tall and strong. "Sit down," she purred in a slurring voice. "I'll dance for you." She started to rise but he stopped her.

"You stay down there. You're so drunk, you'll break your ankle if you try and dance."

Andrea laughed. "I dance better when I'm drunk."

"You get better tips, I imagine," Thomas said. "But not because you dance better."

She gave him a dirty look but couldn't argue. Even a small buzz made her willing to do about anything a customer asked.

Thomas pulled off his shirt and exposed his well-built torso.

Andrea's mouth watered. "So, if I'm not dancing, what am I doing?"

"Take off your panties," he said.

Andrea bit her lower lip, wiggled her hips, and peeled up her skirt. She looked up at the man as she slipped her panties, already wet, down her slim brown thighs. Two forgotten fifties tumbled to the floor, but she would get them later. She was passed caring. She bet forward, still looking up as she slipped the panties down her calves and over her massive heels.

He held out his hand and she placed the balled-up, red lace panties in his palm.

"Open up," he commanded in a firm, gentle voice.

She opened her mouth and Thomas stuffed the panties in, gagging her in lace. She felt a shiver of excitement, tasting the tang of her pussy, the salt of her sweat, and the clean taste of linen. She was dizzy with need. She could see the outline of his massive erection pushing against his slacks. She leaned back, spread her legs and pressed two fingers to her cunt, teasing her lips and clit as she stared up at the tall, handsome man.

He smiled calmly, watching her tease her cunt as he began to slowly undo his slacks.

She wanted to beg him to fuck her, but it just came out as a muffled moan through the lace of her panties.

He slipped off his slacks, his big erection springing free as they dropped to the floor. Her pussy tingled, her hips working as her fingers pressed harder against her desperate cunt.

She moaned again through the wet lace.

Thomas moved onto her, pressing her back on the couch, as he took both her wrists in his hands and pulled her fingers from her cunt. She stretched out lengthwise on the couch, her skirt bunched up at her hips, shaved pussy bare and aching with hot need. She wrapped her legs around the powerfully built man, pulling him closer, her slutty stripper heels pressing against his muscular thighs. He pulled her wrists above her head, then took them both in one of his massive hands, pinning them there as he began to kiss her neck.

She moaned and rocked beneath him, feeling desperate to use her mouth and hands on him, but her mouth was stuffed with panties and her hands were pinned above her head. She wiggled against him as his massive cock pressed against the soft flesh of her inner thigh. He reached down with his free hand and guided his beautiful cock, as more of his weight moved onto her.

Her hands pinned above her head, she inhaled the flavor of linen and her own pussy as she felt the heat of his tip begin pressing against her opening. She tried to pull him in with her heels, but he was taking his time, torturing her with the pulsating heat of his tip.

She arched her back, making her wet cunt more accessible as he continued to tease her, the fat head of his beautiful cock just barely inside her. She was dripping wet, pussy juices running down the crack of her ass and staining the couch beneath them.

He was so calm, looking into her eyes with a cocky smile as she shivered with need beneath his powerful frame.

"Do you want me to fuck you?" he asked.

She answered in a muffled whimper, nodding her head frantically.

"How bad do you want it?" he teased.

She tried to wiggle her body, trying to slide herself beneath his weight and impale herself on his cock, but his hand held her wrists firm, locking her in place. She whimpered again, begging him to fuck her with her eyes. She thought she'd lose her mind if she had to wait another moment for to feel his thick cock throbbing inside her.

His free hand slid up her flat tummy, across her narrow ribcage and then under her lace top and under her bra. He cupped one of her firm tits, nipple hard against his palm. She moaned, heels pressed against his thighs, panties stuffed in her mouth, hands pinned above her head.

Suddenly her whole awareness was overwhelmed with painful, shivering ecstasy as he rolled forward and plunged his massive, throbbing cock deep inside her. She arched against him, her muffled voice high and shaking with need as she felt his thick tool pulsating in her womb. She wanted to cry out, to tell him how amazing his dick was and how good it felt inside her, but instead she just panted into her wet panties and grinded her hips against him.

He moaned with pleasure. "Your cunt is so hot and wet, girl." Then he began to pump his cock inside her, slamming his thick, powerful meat back and forth in her quivering pussy. Her eyes rolled back as his powerful dick rammed back and forth inside her, the contours of his prick massaging her core. He continued to hold her wrists above her head, squeezing her tit as he looked down at her face, slamming his cock mercilessly inside her. She whimpered and shivered, letting him fuck her without the slightest resistance, her slutty heels bouncing against the back of his thighs with every thrust.

"Yes," she whimpered unintelligibly into her panties. "Oh fuck yes!" How had she gone all this time without getting fucked by this beautiful cock?

The powerful man grunted and groaned with pleasure as he continued to hammer her hot, wet cunt. She wanted to reach down and touch him, but he held her wrists firm and she flexed her thin arms helplessly against his strength. Every thrust of his amazing cock thundered through her core, causing shivers and pulses to explode her womb. She forgot where she was and even who she was as the first of several orgasms pulsed through her. She was in bliss, feeling that massive cock hammering inside her. Suddenly he yanked her by her wrists and pulled her from seating and dragged her to an overstuffed chair next to the couch. He released her hands, standing behind her, then with one, forceful maneuver bent her over.

She stood on her towering heels, hair draped over the backrest of the chair, now freed hands pressing against the armrest. He yanked up her skirt and spanked her ass hard with one of his massive hands, the hot, stinging slap sent her rocking slightly forward, a muffled whimper escaping her panty-stuffed mouth. He grabbed her slim waist in one hand, and her sweat soaked blonde hair with another, then rocked back and plunged himself deep inside her once more. She cried out, the angle of his massive tool changing the sensation and sending her spinning into another orgasm. She looked back over her shoulder, eyes wide, mouth stuffed with panties, hair wild and sweaty as the man hammered her cunt.

He held her waist and hair as he smashed her cunt with the force of his massive prick, rocking back and forth inside her soft, wet pussy. The alcohol still swam in her mind, as the cock throbbed in her body, ramming back and forth inside her. One orgasm died down and suddenly built back up, blending into another shuddering intensity. Her slim legs wanted to buckle, but his strong hands and the chair held her up. She could feel his massive cock swelling even more inside her, getting ready to explode.

She whimpered in muzzled cries, eyes pleading, trying to tell him she wanted to eat his cum.

As if he could decipher her muffled words, he grunted, "I'm going to cum inside you. I'm going to fill your slutty, stripper cunt with my hot jizz."

This was why she didn't usually fuck guys in the VIP room. But suddenly, in this blissful state, she couldn't imagine anything hotter than having her fertile womb plowed full of this powerful stud's seed.

"Yes," she told her panties. "Oh, fuck yes."

He slammed himself forward brutally and let out a deep, powerful groan. She could feel the heat and power of his balls shooting into her cunt. Andrea closed her eyes and whimpered into the lace of her panties. She shivered with the remnants of a deep, powerful orgasm, shuddering with every jet of cum that splashed inside her.

Andrea was still tingling with aftershocks of orgasm when she felt him pullout, a trickle of cum running down her thigh. She moaned, aching for the intense fullness that his cock had given her. When she recovered and turned around, he had already gathered his things and left. Andrea spit out her saliva drenched panties and slipped them back on. She pulled down her skirt and smoothed it out, then stumbled out of the VIP room. She took a moment to collect herself. She had been this drunk many times. She smiled and forced herself to concentrate on being graceful and pretty as she strolled across the club. She didn't bother changing her clothes, and instead just grabbed her things from the back room and slipped past the bouncer at the back door.

It was still ten till midnight, but Tim was there, waiting in his car. he hurried out and opened the door for her. "I got nervous," he said. "When you didn't text."

A little dizzy, she dropped into the passenger seat. Was she supposed to text? "Oops," she said. His car was warm and comfortable and everything smelled nice.

"It's okay," he said. "I will always wait for you. You want to go get something to eat?"

"Take me home," she said. She was too drunk to walk around in some all-night dinner, although coffee sounded nice. "To your place," she added. "You can make me coffee."

He didn't joke or complain or imply anything, he just started the car, turned the wheel and started driving.

The drive was a blur, but she had recovered her senses a bit by the time he pulled up his driveway to his small house.

She shifted in her seat, now aware that her panties were still wet from having been in her mouth and sticky from the cum that was running from her well fucked cunt. Tim got out, circled the car, and opened her door. She took his outstretched hand and rose from the seat, focusing so she was controlled and graceful. She concentrated on her walking, barely swaying as she followed him into his house.

As he instantly went to work making her coffee, she marveled at how comfortable his little house was, and how sweet and polite and unquestioning he was. She approached him and when he turned toward her, she pressed herself against him and gave him an enthusiastic kiss, driving her tongue into his mouth. He kissed her back with abandon, then began kissing her neck and shoulder. She shivered with pleasure as his eager mouth showered her with affection. She grinded against him as she led him back. Her ass hit the edge of his kitchen table and she squirmed on top of it, laying back, pushing all his things to the floor.

Instead of moving on top of her, pressing his weight down and claiming her, he stayed standing. He bent over her and began kissing her ribcage and stomach with relentless enthusiasm. Each kiss moved lower, edging towards the waistband of her slutty little skirt.

She thought about stopping him because she knew where he was heading, but she didn't stop him. Andrea had a weakness for getting her pussy eaten. Most guys were terrible at it, yet too conceited and ego driven to take instruction. Sometimes, even though she wasn't into girls, she'd let one of the lesbians at the club go down on her. Tim's gentle touch and tender kisses reminded her of one of those girls. She spread her legs wide, her skirt bunching at her hips, the good hard fucking she'd just gotten making her want the attention of a soft, wet mouth even more. "Yes," she moaned, as he worked his way down, hungry kisses pressing down her to her pelvic bone.

She brought her legs up and lay her thighs across his slim shoulders. She used the leverage to lift her ass off the kitchen table. He dropped to his knees, peeling off her wet, cum-stained panties. Andrea bit her lower lip, her body quivering with anticipation.

He slipped the panties passed her knees, then dipped back forward, pressing his face to the heat between her slim brown thighs.

Andrea left her panties stretched across her calves, knees wide, stripper heels resting on Tim's back. She dug her heels into him, using him for leverage to lift her hips as he pressed his lips to her hot cunt and began kissing her pussy softly. She pressed her hand to the top of his head, feeling his soft hair, moaning, "Yes. That's my boy. That's my good boy."

His gentle kisses and careful licks felt amazing on her well-fucked pussy but she already craved more.

"Yes," she whimpered. "Oh yes, baby," she worked her hips, rubbing her pussy against his face, desperate to feel his gentle tongue inside her. He teased her lips, then dipped his tongue inside her, letting it wiggle in the creamy mess of her well fucked cunt. He let his tongue move inside her for a moment, then he began to lap her up, slurping as he licked her wet pussy.

She felt a flash of guilt, realizing her sweet little pet was lapping up the juices of another man right along with her creamy vaginal fluids, but the moment passed quickly, and a devious thrill took its place. "Yes pet," she moaned. "Yes pet. That's nice. That's a good pet. A little left. Yes. Yes." She used her hand on his head to guide his face to just the right angle.

His eager tongue felt so good, and he took instruction well. He was gentle and careful like a woman, yet eager and hungry like a man. Why should she feel guilty about grinding her pussy against his eager face, just because it was full of another man's cum? They weren't married. He wasn't her boyfriend. It was just a date. He was just a sweet man with an eager tongue. She had never claimed her pussy wasn't dripping with the cum of another man.

"Yes pet," she moaned, her body quivering as she listened to his hungry slurping between her thighs. The memory of that big, hard cock throbbing in her cunt made the sensation of his wet, probing tongue even more intense. She ground her pussy against his face, one hand on the back of his head, her other hand squeezing one of her perky tits. It was the same tit Thomas had been manhandling earlier, and it was a little sore to the touch.

"Eat it," she whimpered, thinking but not saying aloud, 'eat my lover's cum.' "Eat every drop," she whined, her body radiating with intensifying shivers. "My pet, my hungry little pet. Eat it. Eat it all."

He licked, slurped, and swallowed. He lapped at her like an eager dog, desperate for her praise.

"Yes," she whimpered. "Good boy. Good pet."

He continued to lap at her with relentless pace, kneeling on the floor of his kitchen, her heels digging into his back and her hand planted on his head.

"Yes," she cried, rocking against him, panties stretched across her calves. She was grinding herself into his mouth as she felt herself getting closer and closer to ecstasy. "That's my boy. That's my bitch." She shivered with sudden orgasm, the muscles of her long, thin legs pulsating as she shivered. Finally, she relaxed with a long sigh and a satisfied giggle, letting her ass drop back down to the tabletop.

He came up to her, crawling onto the table beside her, his face wet with her juices and another man's cum. "I love you," he blurted.

Andrea laughed, but she kind of felt the same. Warm and tingling in her tummy. Her sweet, adorable pet. "We just met," she scolded him.

"I don't care," he said. "I love you."

"Come here," she said. She pulled him close and cuddled him against her. She could tell he wanted to ask for sex, but he relaxed against her, settling for being pressed against her soft, warm flesh.

She realized then, that she really had found him: The nice guy she'd been dreaming of. Could she be the good girl she told herself she'd become once she finally met him?

"I don't want us to see other people," she said after a few minutes of relaxed silence. "I want to be your girlfriend."

"I haven't even looked at anyone else since we met," he said.

She almost wished she could say the same. She could still feel the heat of Thomas' dick pulsating inside her. But she was glad she had gotten a chance to say goodbye to her slutty life, one last filthy fuck before she became a good, loyal girlfriend. She had to start this relationship with a different tone. She had to start it with purity.

"Let's take things slow," she said. "From now on, let's be good. No sex until we really know each other better, okay?"

"Okay," he agreed with just a slight hint of disappointment.

She pet his head softly. It wasn't exactly purity that made her want to slow down with him. After a while without sex, she hoped, even his small dick would feel amazing. Then, it would be easy to be a sweet and faithful girlfriend. Plus, she couldn't deny, it felt good to make the rules. "Good boy," she purred, and he snuggled closer.

Can't Resist Her Slutty Urges

Andrea rubbed her ass against the man's lap, feeling his massive erection. She couldn't remember what his face looked like. She hadn't gotten a great look at it anyway, not in the darkened corner of the strip club, but the man had a big, fantastic cock. It pressed against her, hard beneath his slacks, throbbing against her bare flesh. One of his big, vein crossed hands moved across her slender torso, as the other cupped one of her perky brown breasts. She was stripped down to her panties in the VIP room, only her slutty stripper heels for adornment as she wiggled herself against the big, strong man behind her.

She was starting to get really horny, and that made her think about her boyfriend. Her boyfriend didn't make her feel like this, but he did make her feel warm, treasured and beautiful. She had always told herself that once she got a good boyfriend, she would be loyal. But, although he was sweet, doting, and cuddly, his touch didn't make her feel like this. They had been together a week already, and she hadn't really slept with him, but she had been faithful. Her secret plan was to give her body time to recover from all the big cocks that she was used to getting fucked with. She believed she could adjust to her new boyfriend's smaller size. She figured after a couple months, she would be a brand-new girl, and his dick would feel as good as anyone's. But it had only been a week so far, and it felt like a very long time. It felt like it had been much longer than she anticipated, and her body was aching to be filled with massive, throbbing cock.

The cock behind her now, even through the fabric of the man's slacks, throbbed with heat and power against the smooth skin of her small round ass. It was the kind of cock she had never even tried to resist before.

As horny as this week had made her, she would have even given in to Tim's small, uninspiring erection, when she felt it pressing against her as they made out on his couch. Yes, if he had pressed the issue, she would have given him some, but he was always perfectly behaved. And the feeling of his thin erection pressing against her, didn't fill her with the pounding, animal need that a cock like the stranger's behind her awakened in her. The only thing she fantasized about, regarding her new boyfriend, was the eager and obedient way he ate pussy. He had no hesitation or restraint, while maintaining his sweet, sensitive demeanor. He took instruction perfectly; softer, harder, left, right, a gentle nudge of his chin, a little yank of his hair; he responded perfectly. Andrea thought about Tim's tongue and felt her pussy tingling even more. She instinctively pushed back against the stranger's lap, driving herself against the throbbing heat of his magnificent cock even harder.

Perhaps she should change the rules with Tim. They could just do oral for a while… but there was a little fear inside her. If she was going down regularly on her boyfriend, would he still be the sweet little pet she found herself falling in love with? Or would he become some regular jerk like the man grinding against her right now?

The man moaned in a deep voice, his hand resting possessively on her thigh. His grip was soft but strong, his hand was coarse against her smooth flesh as he began to slide his touch towards her panties. She spread her legs without thinking, letting his fingers press against the silky lace that covered her cunt.

"Fuck," the man said feeling her through the fabric. "You're wet as hell."

She wondered suddenly if letting herself get fingered by this man would be considered cheating. She was already pressing herself against him, grinding against his cock and his strong fingers. His firm touch pushed her panties back against her hot, wet pussy, lace massaging her clit. She thought about Tim's sweet tongue, as the man's strong hand rested on her pelvis and his thick middle-finger pressed firmly against the thin fabric covering her quivering little cunt. She could feel the heat from his magnificent dick, radiating beneath the softness of her ass. Was she really ready to give up cock like that? Logically, she felt sure she would get used to Tim's smaller dick, and that it was capable, after time, of giving her all the pleasure she needed. But another part of her had become more and more obsessed with big cocks with each day she went without. A deep, primal hunger was radiating in her belly, begging for bigger, more powerful cock. Her boyfriend's sweetness and kind words made her feel content and happy, but she still craved the rough handling and verbal abuse of arrogant, selfish men.

The man beneath her increased the pressure of his finger, rubbing her as she rubbed him. His breath smelled of whiskey and smoke as he moaned across her neck.

Andrea reached behind her, sliding her hand behind her ass, flicking open the top button of his slacks, and slipping her hand under his pants. He moaned when she touched him, and she moaned when she felt his flesh, the heat and power throbbing through the rippled contours of his rock-hard prick. She continued grinding her ass against him, her hand moving with her body, sliding up and down his magnificent cock. The pressure of his finger stopped for a moment, as he slid his hand under her panties. A moment later, one of his fat fingers was wiggling inside her, his hand grinding against her clit, as she stroked and wiggled against his fat, throbbing cock.

Andrea whimpered, grinding and stroking faster as the man's finger pressed back and forth in her wet, quivering cunt.

He came suddenly, with a surprising groan. Hot jets of cum began splattering across her narrow, naked back. Jizz was spraying hot across her flesh and dripping across the little tribal tramp-stamp at the small of her back. Each jet of sperm made her tingle with hot intensity. She was on the edge of her own orgasm as she continued to stroke him, rubbing his dick against her and smearing his cum into the flesh of her back. He finished emptying his balls, and his big cock began to soften slightly, but she continued to use it to smear the warm semen into her flesh. She was so close. She continued to try and ride his finger, but he was done with her. His finger slipped from inside her, making her shiver with aching need.

He pushed her to the side, wiped off his dick on her nearby skirt, and dropped forty dollars on the table. "Thanks, Doll," he said.

As he left the VIP room, she sat a while, cum drying on her back as she fingered herself. But she couldn't get there. She needed more. She needed to get fucked. She decided to go home early. It wasn't the same as getting fucked, but she was going to have Tim go down on her.

She slipped back into her tiny, cum-stained pleated mini skirt and bikini top, then left VIP. She walked through the club, the plaid hem of her skirt swishing across her brown thighs and bouncing against the curve of her little round ass with every step. She slipped into the manager's office to let him know she was leaving.

She saw the man there, sitting with one of the bouncers, passing a bottle back and forth as they laughed about something. The manager was in his early fifties, but had the rugged, handsome build that made him seem timeless and sculpted from stone. The bouncer was in his twenties, built like a spartan warrior, tall and relaxed in his powerful masculinity. As the men turned their eyes on her, she could feel the heat of their gazes, and her tummy tumbled as her pussy flashed with warm heat.

Her manager, Henry, in comfortable dress slacks and a casual button-down shirt, smiled at her. "Your just in time," he said, holding the bottle towards her. "We were just thinking this party could use a feminine touch."

Andrea bit her lower lip. She wanted so bad to touch and be touched.

The bouncer, Gavin, turned toward her, a skin-tight t shirt stretched over his massive torso and loose-fitting jeans belted across his hips. "Come on," he said, using his foot to push a chair that was nearby the little table they sat at. "Join us for a drink."

Andrea didn't even think. She just started walking, swaying as if she was working a client as she slithered over to the chair between them. She took the bottle and took a swig of whiskey, her tummy warming instantly. She held it to Gavin, but he just nodded, and so she took another long swig. She set the bottle down with a smile, her head light, and her body tingling.

"So," Henry said. "Which one of us do you want to fuck first?"

Andrea inhaled. She knew this was going to happen the second she stepped into the room with these two, powerful men, but the shock of having it said so suddenly aloud made her tremble slightly. Any thought of her boyfriend had disappeared from her mind. "Why do I have to choose?" she asked.

"Both at once it is," Henry said with a laugh. "I'd never expect less from my favorite little freak."

Andrea was lightheaded and tingling. She doubted she was her bosses favorite little freak, with all the freaks he had at his disposal. But she was a freak, and she couldn't help it. When was the last time she'd been hammered by two big, beautiful cocks at once? Was it Denise's birthday party, almost a year ago?

She smiled at Henry, then turned and flashed a smile at Gavin. Then, because neither of them seemed to be making the first move, she grabbed her top and pulled it off, revealing her small, full tits, pink nipples hard as pebbles.

A moment later both men's hands were all over her. They scooted their chairs away from the table, as she slipped off her chair and pushed it away. It rolled across the room and banged against the closed door, as she slithered onto the floor on her hands and knees. Both men touched her from either side, Gavin behind her, the bouncer's massive hands feeling her legs and ass. Henry was in front of her, one hand sliding under her to feel one of her tits, the other caressing her blonde hair. Her hands slid off the floor and onto her boss's legs, rubbing him through the fabric as she purred, head moving to his lap.

Henry stayed seated in his chair, relaxing like a king as she caressed his legs with her hands, and the side of her face. Gavin slipped to the floor on his knees, his massive hands, knuckles swollen from street-fights, slipped under her skirt. Gavin took hold of her panties and began to peel them back, sliding them down her thighs.

She began to undo her boss's belt, her ass wiggling back and forth unconsciously, her pussy aching with need.

Henry caressed her hair and squeezed one of her tits as she opened his slacks and pulled out his massive, semi-erect cock. She began to kiss it, licking the tip. She inhaled his powerful musk as she stroked him, messily using her tongue to smear drool across the swelling purple tip. Behind her, two of Gavin's fingers touched her wet slit.

"Fuck," Gavin said. "I love a girl who doesn't need any foreplay. This slut is fucking dripping."

She continued to lick and kiss and nibble at her boss's cock as it hardened against her lips. "I'm ready," she purred to the bouncer behind her. "I need it. Please give me your cock."

Henry laughed, petting her hair like she was a kitten as she slobbered over his thick, throbbing meat. "That's it," he said. "That's my needy little freak."

She rubbed her cheek across Henry's spit covered cock, lowered her face to his balls and began to kiss his balls threw the opening of his slacks. He raised his hips up, allowing her to peel his slacks down to his ankles. She looked back over her shoulder at the bouncer, her panties tight against her knees, her tiny skirt so short it exposed her hot wet cunt in her bent position. "Fuck me," she begged Gavin. "Fuck my little freak pussy. I need your cock. I have a new boyfriend, and his cock isn't enough for me."

Gavin laughed, obviously happy to fill that need. She could see his cock was already out, immense and throbbing in his powerful grip as he knelt behind her, fingers teasing her pussy-lips. She turned forward again; hand still wrapped around her boss's fat shaft. She stroked him as she gazed up at him. She gave him one long, slow lick, from just beneath his balls to the tip of his massive cock. Then she turned her gaze from his face to his dick, and swallowed him down her throat with one, garbled, wet-sounding gulp.

She felt Gavin's naked thighs, thick with muscles and hair, pressing against the outside of her thighs as he moved closer, his hard prick resting against her ass. He rubbed his hands up then down her slim sides, then brought his big hands to her small, curving ass-cheeks. He held her ass, using his fingers to split her cunt apart like a ripe fruit.

Andrea slobbered up and down her boss's fat cock, her blonde hair tickling his thighs, his balls, and her own pretty face. Drool streaked down from her lips and coated his shaft, dripping down his hairy balls and forming a little wet spot in the fabric of his chair. She loved the feeling of her throat being stuffed with delicious cock. Her hands moved up and down the inside of his thighs, fingernails teasing his thick, masculine flesh.

Gavin moved forward, pressing his swollen meat into her open cunt. As the fullness of Gavin's big cock filled her core, she felt the orgasm she'd been so close to earlier, suddenly wash over her. He had barely even penetrated her, and she was already shivering with ecstasy. Unable to focus on throating Henry's big cock, she brought her lips to her boss's tip and stroked his shaft with her hand, cheeks pulling in as she sucked him. Her brain was swimming, and her body was shaking as Gavin finally pushed his cock all the way inside her, her body quaking with every wave of his erections throbbing heat.

Gavin grabbed the waistband of her skirt, bunching the fabric in both his fists and turning it into a belt, or a harness. He eased his cock back, pulling it till just the tip of his powerful dick was inside her, then he used that improvised harness to jerk her body towards him, slamming her back against his thighs and pushing his meat deep inside her quivering womb.

As Andrea jerked back, her boss's cock slipped from between her lips and hovered in front of her face, her hand still jerking it frantically as her body continued to writhe with painful orgasm. She kept her mouth open, tongue extended, saliva dripping from her tongue as it reached for Henry's thick meat.

Gavin used her skirt harness to push her back forward, sending the contours of his cock slipping through the folds of her pussy as his meat slid back. She gobbled up her boss's cock again, slipping him deep down her throat just in time to be jerked off it once more, as she was hammered back, impaled on Gavin's massive prick. She kept her mouth open, wet tongue extending desperately toward the hot meat her mouth craved.

Gavin began to fuck her faster and harder, jerking her back and forth so fiercely that she couldn't hope to get Henry's dick back in her mouth, instead she just licked it whenever it came near, smearing her boss's hairy balls and throbbing cock with saliva and desperate hunger. The cock throbbing inside her pulsated with intensity and power as she continued to shiver and moan with one long, continuous orgasm.

She lapped at her boss's cock like a dog as Gavin plowed her back and forth, slamming her into the other man's spit wet meat. Her long, slutty heels clicked together with every thrust, her panties stretched across her knees, her soft skirt biting into her tummy and waist like a rope, as Gavin used it like a horse's lead, driving her back and forth along the length of his hard, throbbing cock.

"Fuck," she whimpered. "Oh fuck. I needed this. I needed to get fucked like this."

Gavin slapped her ass hard with one hand, his other hand wrapped in her bunched-up skirt, his cock pummeling back and forth inside her. Instead of passing, her orgasm just kept intensifying.

"Yes," she cried. "Oh fuck. Oh, fuck yes. Thank you. Thank you for your amazing cock."

As Gavin pulled her back, he suddenly thrust forward, meeting her halfway with sudden, shocking power. He thrust her forward, smashing her face into her boss's balls as his own balls began to unload. He groaned in orgasm, and she whimpered in high, thrilling ecstasy as he began to fire hot jets of cum deep into her womb.

"Yes," she cried, "Yes," her voice muffled by her boss's spit-wet balls. Oh, fuck yes."

Gavin filled her with so much cum, pumping it inside of her till his balls were drained. He then pulled out of her. She could feel his potent cream running down her thigh as she sighed in blissful relief, gratefully kissing her boss's balls. She raised her head, ready to finish sucking Henry off, but the man had other ideas.

The strong, older man grabbed her under her armpits and picked her up as he stood. Her panties slid down her smooth brown legs to her ankles, and she kicked one foot free, leaving her panties dangling from one ankle as she wrapped her legs around her boss's waist and began to passionately kiss him. She writhed against him, slutty heels crossed behind his back, his thick cock pressing against her belly, cum running down her thigh.

Henry dropped her onto her back on his table, knocking over the bottle, whiskey spilling in her hair. Gavin stepped over, picked up the bottle and took a swig as he watched their boss penetrate her, driving his big cock deep into her already abused cunt.

"Yes," she moaned. "Oh yes."

Her boss stood up, hands on her hips and he began to really drill her. She brought her legs to his shoulders, giving him more leverage, her slutty stripper heels framing his face, her skimpy stripper skirt twisted and bunched at her waist. She looked at the handsome older man, as the man continued to plow her savagely. Her small tits jiggled, ribcage exposed as she stretched across the table, moaning in ecstasy once more.

Henry grunted, fingers digging into her soft brown flesh as he hammered her mercilessly.

"Yes," Andrea cried out, as her body began to shiver with orgasm once more. "Oh, fuck yes."

Henry groaned. "Yes. You dirty little freak. You filthy little slut. Take it. Take it."

"I love it," she cried. "I'm never going to give it up. I was born to be your filthy little slut. I was made to be a dirty little freak. Yes. Fuck me. Fuck me. Yes!"

Her body exploded into another level of orgasm as her boss began to cum inside her. She could feel his seed squirting deep in the depths of her cunt, as the world spun, and her body tingled with heat and ecstasy.

Henry pulled himself from inside her, his dick sliding out of her raw, cum drenched pussy with ease. He dropped to his chair with a satisfied sigh, took the bottle from Gavin and took a big swig.

Andrea sat up, arm across her tits, whiskey wet hair hanging in her face. Henry passed her the bottle. "Good girl," he said.

She smiled. "Thank you," she purred as she took the bottle and downed another swig before gathering up her clothes, only then remembering her boyfriend.

Andrea went back into the dressing room. All around her stunning beauties slithered from one slutty outfit to the next. She took out her phone and stared at it. A text from Tim stared up at her, "Miss you."

Her heart ached. She had always told herself when she met the right guy, she would be faithful to him. She knew now, she was not capable of giving up asshole men with magnificent cocks, no matter how sweet and loving her man. She could cheat on Tim easy enough, she knew lots of girls who did that. But that just wasn't her. She wasn't going to live a lie.

He was sweet, funny, and fun, but Andrea now knew she had to break up with Tim. She sighed sadly and sent Tim a text. "We have to talk tonight. Wait up for me. I'll be over after my shift."

Now that her decision had been made, and the text sent, she felt sad, but a little bit relieved. She didn't have to pretend to be something she wasn't. To celebrate, she decided to go back on the floor and find one more nice, big cock to play with before she'd go breakup with Tim. She needed to make up for lost time.

Can't Resist His Submissive Needs

When she approached the door to Tim's house, she was still a little drunk. Tim had sent her a dozen texts. "What's going on?" "What do we need to talk about?" "Please don't break up with me."

Most of them had been sent at the end of her shift, while she was getting fucked by the third guy of the night. That last guy had been a bald middle-aged chubby guy, but Andrea hadn't cared. She had moved from guy to guy, grinding against laps until she came to the first, big, hard cock she could find. She led the chubby bald man to VIP, and when he asked how much VIP dances cost, she just kissed him. "I just want to have some fun," she had moaned. "Pay me whatever you feel like when were done."

She had pushed the man into the room, pulled his pants to his ankles and sucked him till his hardon was raging. She could hear Tim's texts pinging her phone, but she ignored them. She had decided to deal with her soon to be ex-boyfriend later. At that moment, all she cared about was getting her fill of thick, throbbing cock. She pushed the man onto the couch and slithered onto his lap. She hovered over him, her short, pleated skirt resting on her parted thighs as she pulled her panties to one side, exposing her tight, bald cunt. She closed her eyes as she began lowering herself down. She was already wet and dripping with two other men's cum as she engulfed that thick rod in her hot, messy pussy. She moaned, pulling off her top and throwing it aside, throwing her head back and letting her blonde hair sway down her narrow brown back. She kept her eyes closed, focusing on the sensation of cock and ignoring the man it belonged to as she began to writhe up and down.

The man buried his ugly face in her tits and began to kiss and suckle her hard, pink nipples, his amazing cock pulsating as she slid up and down its contours. She had writhed and moaned on his lap, as his wet mouth nibbled, sucked and kissed her perky young tits. She rested her hands on his shoulders, focusing on his fantastic cock and ignoring the rest of him as she rode him faster and faster. She whimpered and cried, blonde hair whipping her back as his dick pushed her into another intense, shivering orgasm.

She could still feel that cock throbbing inside her, his cum still wet in her pussy and panties. She had never even asked him his name, just whimpered and moaned, riding his big cock until he exploded deep inside her womb. She could feel the man's cum sticking to her panties, or was that her boss or the bouncer's cum? She had been fucked by so many guys tonight, it had to be a record, even for her. She still felt a blissful and deliciously naughty, in spite of her somber mission, to break up with her sweet, doting little pet.

She already had feelings for Tim, but she felt at peace with her decision. She was doing the right thing, letting her little wounded bird back into the world. He deserved a nice, sweet girl. Still, a selfish part of her just wanted to keep him. Part of her wanted to own him while she cheated with all the beautiful cocks she could. She had to do this quick, before that selfish, bitchy part of her took over and trapped this poor boy forever.

The door was unlocked, and she slipped inside. She caught the scent of her own hair, still pungent with whiskey, and she imagined her whole body must smell like sweat and cum. She should have showered before coming, but she couldn't put this off. Every moment she felt herself losing her resolve. She reminded herself why she was doing this. She couldn't be a pure and chaste girlfriend, but she was not going to be one of those girls living a lie.

She had barely stepped inside before she saw Tim hurry into the hallway. He wore neat slacks and a clean t shirt. He was clean and nice looking, with a kind face and a soft, compliant demeanor. He looked at her with needy desperation and dropped to his knees. "Please don't do this. Please don't break up with me."

He was a combination of pitiful and adorable, begging on his knees for her. She felt a hint of thrill at her own power, followed by a flash of guilt. She didn't want to lose this sweet little man, but the tingling heat still radiating in her pussy from a night of reckless fucking, reminded her she could never be an innocent and faithful girlfriend. Not to him. Probably not to anyone.

"I'm sorry," she said. She swallowed. That wasn't the right approach. She shouldn't be trying to let him down easy. That would be just trying to save herself in his eyes. She couldn't be vague and cryptic, that wasn't fair to him. She had to be tough, final and brutally honest, no matter how bad it made her look.

He was crawling toward her on his knees. He reached up and touched the soft flesh of her calf, pressing his head to her soft, bare thigh. Her heart ached. She wanted to comfort him. His hair was deliciously soft against her tender skin as he cried against her leg. "Whatever I did wrong, I'm sorry. I'll do better."

She could not help him with kindness. The only way to set him free now was to be brutally honest. If she made herself look like the good guy, she would always know it wasn't true, no matter what Tim believed. "I cheated on you," she said bluntly.

He kissed her feet, the curve of her instep, her delicate ankle.

"I cheated on you," she said again.

He continued showering her in soft, desperately wet kisses, up her lower leg, the flesh of her calf, the inside of her knee.

"It's not your fault," he said. "Please don't break up with me. Please don't stop being my girlfriend."

She felt a moment of shock. His weak, and pathetic reaction was something she didn't expect. She felt like she should feel revulsion. Wasn't that how girls were supposed to react to weakness in men? But the shock passed as his gentle, desperate kisses moved higher up her smooth, brown legs. She reached down and touched his soft hair. Her pet. Her sweet, sweet little pet.

She swallowed hard and took a deep breath, her back arching slightly without thinking, her legs instinctively parting. His eager kisses felt so good moving up the soft flesh of her smooth, curved thigh. His touch was delicate, but so filled with desperate, thrilling need that she felt herself starting to surrender to the sensation.

No. No. She was too fond of him to lie, and it was a lie to make him think anything but the truth. How many men had she let cum inside her tonight?

"Don't you understand," she moaned. "I just got fucked. I just had some guys big, hard dick, pounding my cunt. Don't you understand?"

"I understand," he said, his mouth moving high up the inside of her thigh.

She moaned, her body shivering at the soft touch after so much rough use. Wasn't he hearing her? Wasn't he listening? "I got fucked," she said, her voice high and breathy. "I got fucked so good and so hard by men so much bigger and stronger than you. I came so hard on their cocks, and they came so hard inside me. I did anything they wanted. I was their filthy little whore." Instead of a confession, it started to feel like she was bragging, and it was making her wet.

His head between her thighs, his breath tickling her through the lace of her panties. "Thank you for telling me. I don't want you to ever have to pretend. I don't want you to ever have to lie. You can tell me anything. I will always forgive you. Just please don't break up with me."

"Fuck," she moaned, swaying slightly, his lips against her panties, his hot breath and the moisture of his mouth caressing her well fucked cunt through the silk and lace. She was somewhere between a whisper and a moan when she asked, "How can you be like this? Where is your self-respect?"

"I don't know," he said, planting a soft, affectionate kiss onto her panties, the pressure of his lips against her well-fucked pussy making her shiver. "But I'm tired of fighting it. I don't care what that makes me. Please don't leave me. I'll do anything."

Andrea swallowed, dizzy with need. She'd been fucked so hard, and cum so many times, where was this sudden need coming from? Why did she crave her sweet, little pet? "Show me," she purred breathlessly. "Show me you're worth keeping."

"Yes," he said, still kissing her pussy. "Anything. Anything."

She stepped away, stripping as she moved to the bed. She lay down wearing nothing but her stripper heels and panties and spread her legs wide. "Come here," she commanded, in a firm but purring voice. "Come show me."

He moved up to the bed, his desperation slightly chilled as his natural obedience took over. It comforted him, she realized, to be taking orders. She'd always loved getting bossed around by strong, powerful men, so why was it wrong for a guy to want the same thing. And more importantly, why was it wrong for her to want to give it to him? Was this something she liked about Tim? Did she like giving orders?

"Hurry up," she ordered.

He hurried, crawling onto the bed with pet-like obedience. Andrea shivered. She loved the way he responded to her.

"What do you want me to do?" he asked as he crawled closer.

"Finish what you started," she said. "Remind me what a good, little pussy-eater you are."

She spread her legs, she could still feel the raw heat of the powerful fucking she got at the club, and she could feel the tickle of the men's potent semen mixing inside her and dripping into her panties.

"Start by kissing my thighs, nice and gentle." She leaned back and closed her eyes as he began to quietly obey. "Mmmmm, good boy," she purred. "Now kiss my panties. Mmmm, yes. Kiss my pussy through the lace. Can you feel how hot I am?"

"Yes," he moaned.

"Shut up. Focus. Kiss my tummy. Then peel my panties off with your teeth. Mmmmm... good boy."

Tim laid gentle, affectionate kisses on her flat, tan tummy. They were like love-pecks, with a tiny flick of the tongue added at the last minute. Andrea inhaled deeply, her chest rising and ribcage expanding as tingles moved up her spine.

Tim tenderly bit the waistband of her thong. Andrea wiggled and used her hands to help him peel her underwear free. She opened her eyes and watched as he diligently squirmed his way down, lowering himself towards the foot of the bed as he brought the lace thong down her long, brown legs. He reached her ankles, teeth clutching her panties as he worked them past her heels. She sucked the tip of her finger then brought it to her pussy lips, wiping them with a light shimmer of saliva. She brought her fingertip back to her mouth and sucked it once more, tasting her own flesh mixed with the salty cream of three other men. She savored the taste, remembering the huge cocks she had cum so hard on just an hour before as Tim began gently and lovingly kissing his way back up her legs. She spread them again, purring.

"Can you really forgive me for being such a slut?" she asked.

He hesitated, his mouth hovering just above her knee. "I'll always forgive you, for anything and everything. Can you forgive me?"

"Forgive you for what?" Andrea asked.

Tim hesitated. "Forgive me for being..." His voice broke. He couldn't force himself to speak it.

"Forgive you for being a little bitch?" Andrea said for him.

Tim nodded, blushing.

Andrea laughed, strangely impressed. "Maybe. If you're a good little bitch. Now get back to work. Those guys fucked me so good, but none of them had your sweet, little mouth." Her finger teased her slit, cum leaking out of her.

Tim bowed his head and returned to carefully kissing his way up her legs. He squirmed up, between her long legs, finally burying his face between her slim brown thighs.

Andrea closed her eyes. She could still feel the heat of all those fantastic cocks throbbing inside her. Tim began to lick and suck her wet, well fucked cunt. Andrea's finger moved to her clit, rubbing herself as Tim's tongue pressed deep inside her, wiggling in her warm depths. The heels of her slutty stripper shoes rested on the mattress, and Tim gripped one of them, holding the heel like a precious thing. His other hand caressed her thigh and hip, and his mouth slobbered and slurped at her pussy.

"Good boy," Andrea purred. "Yes. Yes. Good boy."

Tim's tongue worked inside her as she remembered all the fucking she'd done tonight. She could still feel the sensations of getting hammered by her boss, a bouncer and one of her customers. How hot had it been, getting spit roasted in her boss's office? How deliciously dirty had it been riding that big cock in VIP, not even knowing the man's name as he came deep inside her.

"Yes," she whimpered, writhing against Tim's mouth, getting more and more excited with each flick of his tongue, and each memory of those other men's hot, throbbing cocks. She found herself pressing harder and harder against his mouth, increasing the friction as she smeared his face with her juices, and the juices of three other men. She writhed against him, wanting to fuck his sweet face.

She grabbed Tim by the hair and pulled him in, locking him to her cunt. "Yes," she moaned. "That's my pet. That's my sweet little pet." She rocked hard against Tim's mouth, but it wasn't enough. She groaned, locked her thighs to his face and began to roll her body. He followed her unspoken command, rolling onto his back until she was on top of him. Riding his face now, knees on either side of his head, insteps of her feet hooked under his armpits, stripper-heels scraping his ribcage, she began to grind her pussy down on his eager mouth. She still held his hair in her hands, twisting as she whimpered and writhed above him.

He slurped eagerly beneath her, without a hint of complaint as she humped his face. Andrea moaned with pleasure, her back arching, firm tits raising, fingers buried in his hair. She rocked hard against Tim's mouth, hammering his mouth with her cunt. She wondered for a moment if she was hurting him, then discarded the concern. He was hers. She could hurt him if she wanted to.

"Yes," she whimpered. "My pet. My obedient little pet."

As her body radiated closer and closer to orgasm, a vicious impulse to humiliate Tim even more took over. "Can you taste them?" she moaned. "Can you taste them inside me? They fucked me so good. Can you taste them?"

"yes. I can," he admitted, breathless and slurping, his voice muffled by the weight of her body. The obedient surrender in his voice was electrifying, and her body inched closer to orgasm.

Her smooth thighs pressed tightly against the side of his face as she rocked above him, her hand twisted in his hair. Her body began to quiver and shake. "Good boy," she whimpered. "That's my good, good bitch."

She didn't know why she loved humiliating him and calling him names, but it was a big part of what was getting her off. Tim seemed to accept it eagerly. He didn't hesitate in his task, diligently licking and slurping and sucking, lapping up the salty cream of three other men leaking from her well-fucked cunt. She didn't know if he loved being her little bitch, or if he just accepted it as inevitable, but she felt like she was claiming much more than his mouth, as she rocked above him, grinding her pussy into his face.

"Yes," she cried. "Yes. My bitch. My perfect, obedient little bitch!" She thrashed as she was overwhelmed with orgasm. Her body twitched and spasmed, legs tense, pussy smothering her pet, but he kept licking and sucking even as he struggled to breath. "Yes!" she cried out. "I own you. I own you little bitch."

Finally, the electricity passed, and her body relaxed, she sighed and collapsed to her side, releasing Tim.

Tim took a deep, relieved breath, face wet, erection tenting his slacks.

Andrea laughed joyfully. She was so deeply relaxed. She found herself wondering, had she ever cum this hard from oral sex before? Was it because of the cheating or was it the thrill of possession she felt for her little pet? She looked back at Tim, a little tent in his slacks as he stared at her with needy eyes.

She felt a rush of affection for him. He was so adorably pathetic: His little erection so hard and straining, his eyes so desperate and needy.

She giggled and stretched out, so relaxed from yet another orgasm, the perfect finish to the wildest night of her life.

"Do you believe I'll do anything for you now?" he asked.

She smiled, her body light with relaxation and her skin tingling with a sense of power. "You know, I'm not going to stop cheating on you," she said.

There was a long minute of silence, then he asked. "Does that mean you're still my girlfriend?"

"Congratulations," she told him. "Just don't turn into a regular jerk. Keep being the adorable, obedient pet I adore."

"Should we… can we…" he glanced down at the little hardon poking his slacks.

"I'm pretty tired, Sweetie," she purred. "Maybe you can just jack it in the corner or something tonight?"

He nodded with an adorably defeated look of surrender.

"Thank you," she sighed, feeling relaxed and content in her new-found power.

Tim slunk into the corner, opened his slacks and stared at her slim curved body. The quiet sound of him beating off filled the otherwise silent room, while Andrea stretched out on his bed and drifted off to sleep.

Pegging Her Cuckold Pet

Andrea sent her boyfriend a text. "You don't need to pick me up tonight. I've got a ride." She slid the phone into her little purse, ignoring the ping of his reply. She felt a tremble of heat as she looked up at the college football star. She didn't really follow sports, but everyone around here knew who quarterback David Foster was. The tall blonde male had a handsome smile and a chiseled, perfectly balanced body. "I'm ready to go," she said.

He smiled and spoke with amusement when he asked, "Texting your boyfriend to let him know you'll be late?"

She gave David a wicked smile and a flirty wink. "He's a good boy. He'll wait."

The tall athlete laughed, and his deep, powerful voice gave Andrea thrilling chills. He put his arm around her waist and started guiding her to the front door. She squirmed out of his grip. "Dancers can't leave with customers. I have to meet you at your car, or the club will think I'm a whore."

David once again let out a cocky laugh and spoke playfully. "You're not a whore?"

Andrea felt a little tingle. When a guy like this called her a name like that, it always got her going. She laughed as if it was a funny joke. "Are you offering to pay?"

He just looked at her with a look that said, "Do I look like someone who ever has to pay?"

"I didn't think so," she said. "Pull around to the back door. I'll be right out." She leaned in and pressed her tits to his chest as she turned her face up and kissed his cheek. He pat her on the ass possessively, his big, strong hand feeling amazing on the soft curve that rested beneath the thin fabric of her tiny skirt.

The football quarterback left out the front door and she grabbed some things from the locker room. She headed to the back door without changing her slutty dance outfit. She wore a tiny denim skirt and top that resembled a strip of denim. The strip of faded blue cloth was just wide enough to cover her nipples as it stretched across her firm, young tits. She slipped on a jacket and wore it open over her top. She almost always went home in her slutty dance outfits now, at least, whenever she was going to see Tim after work.

Her sweet little boyfriend always got worked up seeing her dressed so slutty and still so sweaty from the club. He always went down on her, without asking who she danced for, or how far any of those dances might have gone. After eating her out, he would always beg for sex, but she would instead ask him to jack off. Sometimes she would watch him, but usually she'd watch tv or drift off to sleep as Tim jacked it shamefully in the corner or quietly beside her in the bed.

She realized it wasn't a fair way to treat her boyfriend, and at first the meanness of it was an accident. She could at least give him a blowjob or even a hand job as a reward for his enthusiastic oral service, but she was afraid. What would happen to his sweet devotion if she actually gave him sex? But over the last week of regularly denying him, the unfairness of it all had become a turn on all on its own. It had become as much of a thrill as any of the other things she made him do for her. She would moan and writhe as he ate her out for over an hour sometimes, her knowing all the while that she would refuse him even as much as a simple hand job, and that knowledge would make her cum even harder.

He always took the news with disappointment but without complaint, as if he secretly agreed with her decision, but he always had the same hopeful gleam in his eyes the next night when he begged for sex again.

Andrea laughed at herself. She was about to hook up with a famous local stud, and here she was thinking about her sweet little boyfriend without a hint of guilt. She stopped at the back door and checked her phone. Tim had texted her. "You sure? I don't mind picking you up." Then a few minutes later texted. "Okay. See you when you get here. I love you."

She smiled. "Be good," she texted back, then slipped out the back door to meet her stud.

David picked her up in a new Mustang convertible, sleek and red. She slithered into the passenger seat and he skidded out of the parking lot. He drove fast and hard and the loud, powerful response of the car made her gasp and quiver. They had made it just a few blocks when she slipped her knees up onto the seat and bent over the console, head hovering over his lap. He eased his seat back but didn't slow down, gunning down the road, slipping a big hand under her skirt and feeling her smooth, brown ass.

Andrea opened the football stars zipper and tugged at his jeans. He shifted his weight, allowing her to pull his jeans and underwear down just enough to expose his big, semi erect cock. She took it in her hand and kissed it, then gave him a quick lick. He grew hard almost instantly, his fat cock perfectly straight and amazingly built.

"Fuck," Andrea purred, gently stroking him. "If the football thing falls through, you could definitely be a porn star."

His hand squeezed her ass in a possessive and reassuring way as she opened her mouth and wrapped her lips around the fat, purple mushroom head. She slurped wetly, lowering her lips down his pole as he sped down the road, blasting through stoplights.

Andrea slobbered up and down his rock-hard prick, tasting the power of his testosterone as her head bobbed and her ass wiggled in his hand.

Andrea lost herself in the amazing sensation of perfect cock, sliding through her lips, pressing against her tongue and moving through her throat. She savored the feeling of the car speeding around corners and shifting lanes as thick meat moved through her wet mouth.

Suddenly the car eased to a stop. She looked up at him questioningly, cock still in her mouth. He pressed the button on his seat, sliding it back all the way. One of his big fingers caressed the wet spot in her panties, teasing her pussy-lips through the silky fabric.

"Get on my lap," he told her. "I want to feel that wet little pussy."

She sat up, reached under her skirt and wiggled out of her panties. She tossed her panties aside and straddled him, facing his handsome face as she lowered herself on his powerful, throbbing cock.

She moaned as she engulfed his massive tool in her soft, wet cunt. They began to kiss, tongues wiggling into each other's mouths as she began to writhe on his lap, sliding her body up and down his meat. The football star's strong hands moved up and down her body, feeling her slim sides and the curve of her ass as she whimpered, riding him.

David moaned in the moments between their frantic kissing, "Oh fuck yes. You're pussy's so good."

"Your cock is amazing," Andrea purred into his mouth.

She rode him faster, grinding against his lap, as he used his powerful abs to thrust back into her.

The athlete's strong hands moved up and down her body, squeezing her ass, and her tits as she writhed on his throbbing meat. "I love it," she moaned. "I love your big cock. I love your strong hands."

His grip tightened as he moaned, his cock swelling even more inside her.

Andrea purred into the football stars ear, whimpering as his big dick drove back and forth, deep inside her. She kissed his ear and licked his face, moaning as her body began to shiver with growing ecstasy. She thought about Tim, waiting for her at home, and it pushed her over the edge.

"Oh fuck," she moaned into the football star's ear. "Oh fuck. Your cock. Your amazing cock." She began to shudder with bliss as she was rocked with orgasm.

The feeling of her ecstasy pushed him over the edge as well and he began to explode inside her, filling her womb with streams of hot, potent sperm. She hugged the stud closer, her body light and tingling, her tits mashed against him as she kissed him frantically.

Her body shivered as his balls emptied inside her and his tongue wrestled hers.

Finally, as his dick finished twitching and began to soften slightly, she slid off him and moved back to the passenger seat. She found her panties but before she could put them back on, David said, "Put them in the glove-box. I like to keep a souvenir."

She opened his glovebox and saw it was stuffed with girl's sexy panties of different styles and sizes. Andrea laughed as she pushed her panties into the mass, "Naughty boy." It was cute, and kind of charming that this young stud was such a bad boy, but she was glad she had a good, loyal boy at home. She smiled at the thought of Tim. Tonight, she was going to give him a special surprise.

David pulled in front of Tim's house a few minutes later, and she gave the football star one last kiss before sliding out of his car. She stood up and tugged on her skirt, self-conscious about not wearing panties, cum running down her thigh. She waved goodbye to the football star as he drove off, and she walked up to David's door.

He had given her a key, but the door wasn't locked, so she walked into his house.

He was still awake, and he hopped up as she walked into the living room. His eyes went up and down her slim, curving body, thrilled by her slutty little skirt, massive heels and slinky top. She slipped off her jacket to show off her slender torso and her firm tits, packed tightly by the narrow top.

"Hi Sweetie," she purred. She loved how nervous she still made him.

"Hi," he said.

She moved closer, strolling on her heels, slow and predatory. "Aren't you going to ask me about my night?"

"How was work?" Tim asked her.

"You know David Foster?" Andrea asked, unable to hide her giddy smile.

"The football player?" there was a hint of star-struck excitement on Tim's face.

Andrea nodded. "He just fucked me."

Tim's face turned shocked. "You… you were with another guy again?"

Andrea had fucked at least one other guy every day since they started dating, but she hadn't bothered to mention every single one. She just assumed it was understood. If he really wanted to know, all he had to do was ask.

"Not just another guy," she purred in a flirty, teasing tone. "A famous guy." She moved even closer to her little pet. "He had an amazing dick."

Tim was speechless, but also mesmerized, looking at her in her slutty little outfit, leaning closer, inhaling her scent.

Andrea stopped when they were an inch from touching and purred, "It wasn't just big. I fuck a lot of guys with nice, big cocks, but his dick was so perfectly shaped and so hard and strong. It sucked him so hard, it felt so nice in my throat."

Tim closed his eyes, swaying, a tent forming in his slacks as he pictured it.

Andrea laughed at her pet, leaning in, letting her tits press against his chest, purring into his ear. "I rode him in his car, just now. My pussy sliding up and down his big, hard cock while you were waiting for me. He came so hard in my cunt, and I came hard from his amazing dick. But I came even harder from knowing you were right in here, obediently waiting." She kissed his cheek.

Tim, eyes still squeezed shut, swallowed hard. His body swaying, thin erection throbbing in his pants.

She reached down and caressed him through his slacks. "Mmmmm," she purred feeling his hard dick. "Someone is so turned on. My little pet loves hearing about me getting fucked by other men, doesn't he?"

He stuttered, his voice full of shame, his brain unable to answer.

"It's okay," she purred. "I can tell it turns you on."

"I wish it didn't," he confessed.

Andrea purred in his ear, flicking her tongue across his earlobe. "You can't help what you are."

"It does turn me on when you're bad," he admitted. "I wish I was normal, but I'm a freak."

She pressed her palm harder against his slacks, laughing as she rubbed him up and down. "You're not a freak. You're MY freak."

"I want that to be true. I want to belong to you."

"It's true," she said. "Take off your clothes and sit on the edge of the bed. I have something special for you."

She could see him shaking with nervous excitement as he stripped eagerly and hurried to the bedroom. He sat down on top of the blanket at the edge of his comfortable mattress.

Andrea followed him into the room. She started swaying like she was on the dancefloor, teasing him as she moved closer. He was shaking with expectation, his breathing heavy and his eyes mesmerized by her slinky form. She moved in front of him and used her leg to push his knees apart, then knelt between his legs. He was rock hard, his naked body shivering with expectation. She slithered out of her top, exposing her perky, naked breasts, nipples hard and pink.

. "Tell me I can do anything I want to you." She commanded.

"You can," he moaned. "You really can. I just want to be your pet. I'm tired of pretending to be like other guys. I've tried fighting my weak, submissive nature all my life. But I was born to be a pet, created to be your loyal eager pet."

Andrea purred, "I've never tried to fight my dirty, slutty nature, I've always surrendered to every filthy impulse eventually, but I'm so glad I don't have to start being a good girl now. I'm so glad we can both be ourselves together."

"You can be anything you want with me. You can do anything you want to me."

"We are perfectly matched," Andrea purred, her smooth naked sides rubbing against the inside of Tim's thighs. "A mean, slutty girl, and her eager little pet."

"You're not mean. You're perfect."

She giggled, "Good pet," she purred. "But I am mean. And I'm going to get meaner. Promise me you will always be sweet, eager and obedient."

"I will. I promise."

She leaned over his dick and spit, dropping a huge glob of saliva onto his thin prick. She took a loose grip of his shaft, smearing spit all over his little rod. Her other hand slipped into her purse and pulled out a large, realistic dildo.

He looked at it, big and bulging with artificial veins. His eyes were wide. "What's that?" he asked.

She ignored the question and pushed the huge toy against his erection, smearing it with spittle as she rubbed the cool silicone against his rod. She spit again, this time on the head of the dildo, the spittle dripping down like icing on the massive dong and dribbling over his little erection.

"I'm going to fuck you with it," she said, holding the big fake dick by the fat, artificial balls.

He started to speak but she shushed him, rubbing his dick and the much larger toy against each other, both dripping with drool. "This dildo has gotten me off so many times. I can't wait to get you off with it."

Again, he tried to speak. "I'm not…" but again she shushed him.

"Do you want your first time hard and rough, or soft and gentle?" she asked, smiling wickedly, his little dick still hard against her toy.

"I… I don't know if I'm ready for this." His voice was dripping with delicious fear.

"You're ready," Andrea purred, slipping the wet tip of the dildo down his balls, across his taint and teasing it between his ass cheeks.

"I don't know," he said.

"I know," Andrea purred, twisting as she pushed the toy through his cheeks, bringing the fat, mushroom tip to his tight, virgin asshole.

"I'm not sure I want this," he said, squirming adorably.

"I'm sure I want it," Andrea said, smiling at her nervous pet. "That's what matters right? You promised me obedience. It's not really obedience if we only do things you want to do."

"I guess so," he said, whimpering.

Andrea laughed. "Good boy. Now stop squirming. This is going to happen, but if you relax, I think you're actually going to like it."

Tim stopped squirming and bit his lower lip, whimpering as she began to penetrate his tight little rectum with her huge toy. She loved the weak little sound he made as the tool drove into him. She felt another rush of power, like she was claiming him in some way that went beyond all the things she'd already done. All the amazing orgasms she'd gotten from all the big-dicked studs she had ever fucked had never given her this intense rush of powerful, vicious energy.

"Good boy," she purred.

"It hurts," he whimpered.

She eased the toy deeper. "It's okay," she said. "You'll get used to it."

He whimpered again, his voice so weak and broken. His dick had softened, and was limp against his pelvis, resting in a puddle of her spit. She took her free hand and smeared the spittle across his dick, massaging his limp dick and balls as she eased the toy back, easing the pressure in his rectum. She could feel him getting hard again against her palm as she began to drive the dildo carefully back and forth inside his tender anus.

He was fully hard again, but still whimpering. "It hurts."

"Tell me what a little bitch you are," she purred, lightly massaging his dick as her toy wiggled deep inside his sphincter.

"I'm a bitch," he whimpered. "I'm a weak little bitch."

"Mmmm," Andrea purred, savoring the breaking sound of his voice as her toy twisted back and forth inside him. "Tell me how grateful you are to finally be getting fucked like a bitch."

His dick was throbbing against her palm now, and she began to gently stroke it once more.

"I'm so grateful. I'm so glad to be getting what I deserve."

"Good bitch. You deserve this pain, don't you sweetie?" she began to drive the toy back and forth a little harder.

"Yes," he whimpered, his dick throbbing, his breath hard and panting, voice high, betraying the pleasure pulsating beneath his pain. "Yes. I deserve it. I'm a little bitch and I deserve to be fucked like one."

Andrea felt so turned on. She could feel the heat radiating inside her as she began to plunge her toy back and forth in her boyfriend's ass even harder. "Mmmmm, fuck baby," she purred. "You so bring out the vixen in me. I've never been such a cruel, cruel bitch before. I love this feeling."

Tim was whimpering, his voice full of confused pleasure and throbbing pain as she claimed his asshole and stroked his spit-wet cock.

"Tell me you love it. Tell me you love it when I'm cruel to you." Her firm, ripe tits jiggled as she jammed her toy back and forth inside him with one hand and jerked his little cock with the other.

"I love it," he cried, voice breaking, heart pounding, dick throbbing. "I love it when you're cruel. I love finally getting treated like the bitch I am."

"Never change, little bitch. Never stop being my obedient, desperate little pet."

"I won't," he cried, his voice breaking with pain and ecstasy. His ass on fire and his dick beginning to twitch in her hand. "I'm your obedient pet. Forever." He let out a high-pitched cry, her toy buried in his rectum, as he began to cum in powerful jets. His thin wads of spunk splattered against the ceiling and the dresser across the room as Andrea laughed in delight. Tim shuddered, ass quivering on her toy, his dick shooting out the final sputters of his orgasm onto his tummy.

She giggled, wiping her fingers on the blanket beside him. She stood up, her curved body brushing against the inside of his thighs as she rose, leaving her toy buried to the balls in his rectum. She kissed him on the forehead and purred "Clean up your mess, Sweetie. I've got to go get my stuff. I've decided that I'm moving in."

He whimpered; the toy still buried inside his twitching asshole. "Give me a minute. I'll come help," he said.

Andrea laughed again. "Wait here sweetie. Rest that ravaged little asshole. I think you'll be sore for quite a while. I broke you in pretty hard." She gave him a sweet smile and a pat on the thigh before she walked into the other room.

Andrea would only be grabbing a few essentials tonight, so she didn't need help. Besides, pegging Tim had got her so turned on, that she had a detour to make. She grabbed one of Tim's t-shirts and put it on, then looked in the mirror. She adjusted her outfit and checked her makeup before slipping her phone out of her purse and sending a text to a lover she hadn't seen in weeks, offering to stop by his place. She smiled when he texted back immediately. She was going to get herself another nice, hard cock to finish off this filthy day. She didn't bother putting on panties as she slipped out the door on her way to get fucked again.

The Cuckold's Party-Girl

Andrea looked at her adorable little man. He was nervous. He'd probably never been to a party full of so many beautiful people. It was a birthday bash, put on by one of the dancers at her club. Many of the girls had hot studs for boyfriends or dates, but an equal amount had lesbian lovers just as delicious and electrifying as them. The last segment of hot strippers at the party, probably had sugar-daddies or even little cucks like Tim, but they had left them at home and were flirting their way through the crowd, looking for someone to go home with.

There were also DJs, bouncers, and musicians. It was the kind of party sweet little Tim had only fantasized about. Hot drunk and stoned girls stumbled around half dressed, open doorways showed rooms where wanna-be starlets blew low-budget movie producers, or slinky young strippers 69ed each other. Tim was practically trembling. Andrea gave his hand a comforting squeeze and smiled at him. "It's okay," she said. "You're here with me. You're mine. And nobody ever hurts my things."

Tim nodded, slightly comforted but still visibly nervous. Andrea nodded back at him and began to lead him into the crowd.

Andrea pulled him along by his wrist, swaying in front of him in her slinky black dress. The dress was short and strapless. It looked like one wrong move could cause it to slip off and fall to the floor, leaving her slim, curved body completely exposed. She towered over her boyfriend in her massive platform heels as he followed behind her like a nervous, reluctant pet.

She brought him into the main room of the party, the ballroom of a mansion that belonged to someone's rich "uncle". She pulled Tim next to her, draped herself over him. She could feel the electric reaction in his body, as he felt her silky skin brush him, and her lustrous blonde locks drape over him. She looked around, scanning all the powerful males moving in the room.

"Sweetie," she asked her boyfriend in a soft, purring tone. "Who do you want me to fuck tonight?"

She could feel him squirming deliciously, caught between arousal and shame. Finally, he spoke. "Maybe, tonight, you and me could…"

"Don't worry," she purred, ruffling his hair. "I'll put your sweet little mouth to work tonight. I'm going to make love to your tongue for hours, but I still want to fuck. Who do you want me to fuck?"

She could feel him looking around, eyeing all the guys in spite of his embarrassment. "I understand if you have to… I just wish you wouldn't…"

She laughed and gave him a playful bump with her hip, making him side-step slightly. "Don't play coy with me. We both know I'm going to fuck another guy tonight, and we both know you're going to enjoy it." She pulled Tim close again and hugged him as she looked around. "What about him. The one in the black t shirt. He is going to have a fantastic cock."

"How… how can you tell?"

"Girls can always tell, Sweetie," Andrea purred into Tim's ear. "One glance and we can size guys up, all the way up from porn-star level and all the way down to… well… you."

There it was again. That mean streak that Tim brought out in her. She reached down and touched Tim's crotch, reassuring herself as she felt his erection stirring. "So, who's it going to be?" She purred. "This party is full of studs. Which one am I fucking tonight?"

Her sweet, shy boyfriend didn't speak, but he did look around, and his eyes kept drifting back to one man. It was an older, tall roguish looking man. He was in his late forties, with greyish brown hair, a full, perfectly groomed graying beard and a lean, long torso. His handsome face was chiseled and worn. He had powerful hands and forearms that looked like they were earned from hard work, and his timeless muscular body looked like it was earned from athletic, outdoor living instead of a gym.

Andrea purred, following his gaze as it returned to the man again. "Good choice, Sweetie. How did you know I liked the Daddy types?"

Tim didn't speak. He just stood, turning slowly red, his erection poking his slacks. Andrea bent at the waist, her short dress rising as she kissed her boyfriend on the cheek. "Have fun," she purred. "But behave. I'll text you when I'm done. Wish me luck."

She walked a few steps then turned and looked back at Tim. "Wish me luck," she repeated more firmly.

"Good luck," he whispered.

She smiled and blew him a kiss. "Good boy." Then she turned, swaying deliciously as she walked toward the handsome older man.

Andrea moved up behind the man, and then to his side. She pressed her body against his solid frame, inhaling his masculine scent as she ran a hand across his strong chest. "Hi Daddy," she purred.

When the man looked at her, she pretended to be embarrassed. She laughed and buried her face in the meat of his shoulder. "Oops," she said. "I thought you were someone else." But she made no hint of moving away. He wrapped an arm around her, his powerful stature pulling her even closer in a warm and comforting way.

"What a lucky guy he must be," the man said, his voice deep and steady. The man's strong hand rested casually on the curve of Andrea's slender back. The man seemed immensely experienced, and he had a natural, relaxed masculinity that seemed more powerful than any of the thick, muscle-bound stud's she'd ever fucked.

Andrea could feel Tim watching from across the room as she purred, "He could have been lucky... but I guess he must have gone home. I can't find him anywhere."

The older man's touch drifted down her back, his hand big and powerful as he gave her small, rounded ass-cheek a firm but gentle squeeze. "He must be somewhere. Perhaps I can help you look for him."

"Okay," Andrea purred. "Where should we look?"

She gave Tim a smile and a wink from across the room as the older man started guiding her away from the crowd, his hand resting on her butt, the hem of her short dress pulling up under his grip to reveal the sharp curve of her thin brown thigh as it arched up to her full curving ass.

The older man led her into an empty bedroom and closed the door behind him. Andrea breathed in the man's masculine scent once more, then stepped away and turned to face him, smiling wickedly.

"I'm Ed," the older man said. His voice clear and strong, with a hint of hard living beneath it.

"Andrea," she replied, and gave the man a small little curtsy.

He looked her up and down. "You are a cute little thing," Ed said.

Andrea took hold of her dress, and pulled it up, lifting it over her head, then throwing it to the side. She stood there now, platform stripper heels, black lace panties and no bra, her firm young breasts brown and capped in pink. "Only cute?" she asked.

"Getting cuter by the minute," he said. "Come here."

She obeyed, moving up to the older man, her body tingling from the power of his attention.

He grabbed her ass with both hands and began to kiss her. She melted against him, his tongue driving into her wet mouth. She grew dizzy with the solidness of his stature and the power of his lips. He lifted her firmly by the ass, his fingers wrapping around her ass-cheeks and resting torturously near her already wet cunt. She wrapped her legs around him, sucking on his tongue. She wiggled her body against him, bare tits pressing against the soft fabric that covered his chest, the lace that pressed against her hot, wet cunt grinding against the growing bulge in his slacks.

She slurped hard on the older man's tongue, sucking it like it was her boyfriend's neglected little dick. Ed carried her across the room and dropped her down on a bed. She could smell cum. They weren't the first ones to fuck in here tonight.

She wiggled across the mattress on her back, wearing nothing but heels and panties. She cupped her perky tits and squeezed them as Ed began to strip.

She shivered with need, watching the man standing beside the bed begin to strip with casual, tortuous slowness. His body was lean and strong, his skin leathery and tough, brushed with thick, grey and black hairs. Andrea watched him undo his shirt, button by button, then slip it off. She salivated as he undid his belt, slipped it free then rolled it and set it on the dresser. He kicked off his shoes, then took off one sock then the other, pressing them into the shoe itself.

Andrea moaned and moved to her hands and knees. She couldn't take it anymore. She crawled to the edge of the bed, grabbed the waistband of Ed's slacks and pulled him closer. She unbuttoned and unzipped him and jerked his slacks down. His big erection pushed against his silk boxers. She kissed the silk, looking up at the older man, then pulled his boxers down as well. She couldn't wait to taste the older man's big, hard dick, and she quickly took him into her wet little mouth, drooling across the tip. Her saliva dribbled past her lips and ran down his thick pole as her cheeks pulled in and her tongue encircled his mushroom head.

The man was calm, watching her as she took more of him into her mouth, pressing him to the opening of her throat. He didn't lose control. He didn't gasp or shiver or moan. He didn't reach down and start groping her. He just watched, his breathing deep and steady and his impressive cock throbbing and hot.

She took him into her throat, feeling her esophagus swell with meat as he finally let out a deep, pleasure filled moan. "Good girl," he said.

She began to drive his throbbing member in and out of her throat, blonde hair waving, lips smacking and throat gurgling.

He finally touched her hair and one of her shoulder blades, his strong hands comforting as she slobbered back and forth along his fat tool.

"That's right," he moaned. "Just like that. Show Daddy what a good girl you are."

She continued to slurp on the man's dick, but she slowed her pace, fighting the urge to make him cum. She wanted him to explode in her mouth so she could feel the approval in his voice and taste the power of his potent seed, but she also wanted to make this last.

He moaned, petting her blonde hair as her had bobbed slowly, his big dick massaging her throat. She wiggled her ass as she knelt on her hands and knees at the edge of the bed. She sucked him slow and easy, savoring the taste and feeling of his massive dick moving across her lips, tongue and the opening of her throat. Finally, she slipped her lips from his pole and looked up at him. She pressed her chest to his meat, stroking him against her bare tits with one hand as her other hand caressed his hairy thigh. "Daddy," she purred. "I could suck your big dick all night if you'd let me. But I really, really need to get fucked. Can you please fuck me?"

He reached down and cupped her face. His hand, guiding her by her jawline, gently pulling her up to her knees. They were nearly the same height now, him standing, her on her knees on the bed. He bent forward and kissed her. He continued kissing her as his strong hand moved up her sides, feeling her curving hips and slender ribcage. He then began to twist her with his hands, turning her till she was facing away from him. He kissed her ear and the side of her neck, as one of his arms moved across her chest brushing against the hard nipples of her firm tits. His other hand reached down and felt the wet spot in her panties, teasing her pussy through the lace. She could feel his hard, hot, saliva covered erection pressing against her back.

"Fuck," she moaned. "Oh fuck, Daddy. I'm so ready. I'm so ready for you to fuck me."

She expected him to bend her over, but instead he pulled her up, lifting her knees off the mattress. She hooked one arm behind her head, holding the back of his neck, as her other hand reached down between her own legs. She pulled her panties aside, exposing her wet cunt to the older man's fingers. She felt dizzy and light, held up so easily by the powerful older man. She hooked the instep of her feet behind his thighs, her stripper heels clacking against each other as she was suspended over the older man's rock-hard prick by the strength of his arms and the friction of his lean, stable body. She gripped the back of his neck, flexing her arm to help support her weight as his free hand moved from her pussy to his own, thick tool. She whimpered with need, spreading her cunt with her fingers as he eased her down. Rolling his hips, he began to penetrate her cunt from behind, arm mashing down on her tits, lips pressed to her long neck.

She whimpered as the older man's fat cock began to slide inside her. She rubbed her insteps up and down the backs of his thighs, slutty platform heels clacking together. She held tight to the back of his neck, arching her back, ass against his lap, tits against his strong arm, head pressing back over his shoulder.

Her body began to shake as his dick buried deep inside her. She turned her face and began to kiss the older man once more, his tongue pressing between her glossy red lips. She gyrated against him, as he rolled his hips, pressing his fat cock back and forth inside her.

"Yes," she whimpered. "Oh yes, Daddy. Fuck yes."

Their tongues continued to pass back and forth between their mouths as she whimpered and writhed against the solid frame of the strong, older man. She felt like a tiny thing in the older man's grip, light and wispy and easy to play with. She rocked harder against him, grunting as his dick slid back and forth in the hot, wet sleeve of her cunt.

She continued to hold the back of his neck, as her other hand rested on the lace of her panties, fingers reaching down to stroke the hardened bead of her clit. She shivered with pleasure as the contours of thick cock moved inside her. She curled back against his cock in a slow, steady rhythm as he hugged her into him and rocked himself into her.

The older man moved forward now, easing her down onto the bed. He pressed her down onto the mattress, his big cock still impaled deep inside her. She lay on her stomach on the bed, one of her arms beneath her, fingers rubbing her clit, her other hand releasing his neck and stretching out to grab the already cum stained comforter. His arm still wrapped around her chest, mashing her tits between her body and the mattress as his weight came down on top of her.

"Yes," she moaned. "Oh fuck. Yes, Daddy."

He kissed and nibbled the back of her neck as he began to rock and grind into her with a faster pace. She felt smashed between his weight and the mattress, his dick beginning to move inside her with more speed and pressure, her pussy tingling.

"Fuck me," she whimpered. "Fuck me."

He began to fuck her harder now, his deep voice grunting with exertion and with pleasure as his big cock thrust back and forth deep inside her. He slid his arm from underneath her, letting her tits, hot and sweaty, press down against the soft fabric of the cum-stained comforter. His weight centered on her ass as his upper body arched up slightly and he began to kiss the back of her spine.

"Yes, Daddy," she whimpered. "Oh, fuck yes."

She could feel his sweat dripping down on her, as he rocked into her harder and faster, her body writhing beneath him. She felt shivers of electric intensity moving in her womb with every thrust of the older man's big, hard cock. Her finger worked beneath her, rubbing her clit as her pussy was plowed by the man's fat tool.

Her feet still hooked behind the man's strong thighs, her slutty heels clicking faster with every thrust.

"Good girl," he groaned. "Good little doll."

"Yes," she cried out, loud enough for the whole party to hear. "Yes Daddy. Fuck me! Fuck me! Your dick is so good!" She felt tingles moving all over her body. Her muscles began to spasm, as if they were tightening with the power of unreleased sexual energy.

The handsome older man grunted like an animal behind her, his voice full of lust and pleasure. "I love it," he groaned. "I love your hot, little cunt."

"Fuck it," she cried. "Fuck my hot little cunt with your big, amazing cock! Fuck me! Fuck me! Yes!" Her whole body began to explode with pleasure as the muscles spasmed faster, her entire frame seeming to throb with tension and ecstasy.

The man groaned, his dick swelling as her cunt spasmed around his girth. He pulled her toward him, arching her back as he smashed down hard into her and began to explode inside her. Hot jizz flooded her womb as she shivered in orgasm.

Her mind spun, her eyes closed, and she suddenly pictured her boyfriend, waiting obediently in the next room and it made her orgasm intensify even more. She saw flashes of color and light as her body tingled from her forehead to her toes. The intensity grew to an almost unbearable level, then began to taper and finally pass.

She rocked against the solid body of the older man, whimpering, her heels clicking as he rocked against her with slow, deep thrusts, milking the last squirts of cum into her fertile, young cunt.

"Yes, Daddy," she moaned. "Oh, fuck yes, Daddy."

He collapsed onto her back, sweaty and panting. She stretched out beneath his comforting weight, feeling alive and recharged, her arms stretching out. Ed pulled out from her now, taking some of his cum with him, carelessly smearing it across her thigh as he withdrew. He rolled off her and pat her ass affectionately with one of his powerful hands as he sat up on the edge of the bed.

Andrea squirmed over him, head over his lap. She looked at his semi erect cock, covered in vaginal fluid and smeared with semen, glistening in the light. She took him in her mouth, gently sucking him clean. She eventually slipped him out of her mouth and began to lick his balls, lapping up the wet streaks where her juices had run down and coated him.

He pet her hair. "Good girl," he said.

Satisfied he was clean, Andrea lay her head on his lap, blonde hair covering his wet cock and balls as she enjoyed his soft, approving touch.

The older man sat over her, caressing her shoulder and her waves of lustrous hair as she rested her head on his thigh.

"That was wonderful," he said. "I'm going to get dressed now. You want to come have a drink? You need a ride home?"

She kissed the thick flesh of the older man's thigh, savoring his scent. "Thank you for offering, Daddy. But I'll just call my boyfriend to come get me."

Ed laughed in a gentle, non-judgmental way. "Okay, Doll. Have fun." He gave her ass a playful slap then stood up, got dressed and left her alone in the bedroom. Andrea rolled over, got her purse and got out her phone. It was time to send for her cleanup boy.

The Cuckold Cleanup Boy

Andrea lay on the bed in just her panties and platform stripper heels. She had just gotten a fantastic fuck from a handsome older man while her sweet, obedient boyfriend waited somewhere in the party that was raging in the rest of the house. She got her cellphone and sent a message to Tim.

"Are you behaving?" she teased. "You better not be talking to girls."

"I'm not talking to anyone," he texted back. "I'm just waiting for you."

"Good boy." She was about to tell him to come find her, when she noticed a young, drunk stud had stumbled into the room. She tossed her phone aside and smiled at the well-built young man. She sat up on the bed, using her biceps to squeeze her perky young tits together.

"Hi there," Andrea purred.

The man walked into the room, still athletic even with a drunken sway to his step. "Hey gorgeous," he said. He walked up to her as she sat on the edge of the bed. He didn't hesitate to reach down and touch one of her firm, little breasts. "You're fucking hot," he said.

She smiled up at him, reaching forward and caressing his crotch. He had a big cock, already swelling in his shorts. She caressed him through his shorts, as he squeezed her tits. Andrea bit her lower lip and stared up at the handsome young man for a minute, as he grew harder beneath her soft, caressing hand. "You're fucking hot," she said.

He moaned, his big dick pressing against his shorts as her fingers trailed up and down it, his hands squeezing her tits, fingers digging into her silky flesh. She finally pulled down his shorts and underwear. His thick, veiny cock sprung free. She took it in her hand, squeezing it as it throbbed with blood. She stared at the magnificent rod, gently stroking it.

She turned her eyes up at the man, staring into his eyes as she wrapped her lips around his tip and sucked him into her mouth. Her head began to bob, blonde hair swaying as she started stroking him and sucking him at the same time. He moaned with pleasure, one hand moving up her back, the other caressing her soft, blonde hair. She began to bob her head faster, her fist pumping, jerking him into her mouth.

"Oh shit," he moaned. "Fuck. Who the fuck are you?"

She slipped him from her mouth, looking up at him with a wicked smile. "I'm just a girl," she said, rising to her knees, her body pressing against him. "I love good cock, and I crave hot cum."

She could feel him swelling even more in her fist, getting close to bursting. She stroked him hard and fast, smacking his fat, purple tip against the hard pink nipple of her left breast.

"Oh fuck," he moaned. "Oh fuck. Don't tell my girlfriend, okay?"

"Okay," she said. "But you sure you don't want to call her in here? I don't mind and audience."

"Oh fuck," he moaned. "You're so dirty. I wish she would be into that. Fuck."

"That's okay," she purred. "Maybe my boyfriend can watch?"

He didn't respond, just caressed her hair and her shoulder, moaning.

She could tell he was already so close. With her free hand, she pulled up his t-shirt. He had nice, strong abs. She began to kiss and lick the ridges of his ab muscles as she stroked him frantically, smacking her tits with his spit-wet cock.

"Fuck," he moaned. "Oh, fuck yes. You're a dirty slut. You're such a dirty slut."

"Mmmm," she purred, kissing his stomach, jerking him against her tits. "I am a dirty slut. After you cum, I'm going to call my boyfriend in here and tell him about all the guys I fucked, while he eats my pussy and tells me how much he loves me."

"Fuck. You dirty bitch. You filthy whore."

She felt his cock begin to throb and bent down so she could take him back into her mouth. She sucked his tip as she continued to jerk him. He began to cum, the first hot spray of jizz filling her mouth with the salty flavor of his musky seed. She pulled him from between her lips and straitened up, pointing him at her chest. She purred against his stomach, still jerking him as he continued to spray all over her small, round tits.

"Come on my tits," she moaned. "Cum all over my tits."

He was groaning as he unleashed wad after wad of filthy spunk all over her perky young breasts. Finally, when he'd unloaded his balls, she smiled up at him, her tits dripping with cum, a little cum running down the side of her mouth. She pulled up his shorts for him and gave his ass a pat. "You better go find your girlfriend," she said.

He hurried out of the room as she picked up her phone and sent Tim a text. "Come find me. You better hurry before I get busy again. I'm in the third bedroom on the right."

She was surprised by how quickly he arrived. He must have been lingering nearby, just waiting for permission to come to her.

"Good boy," she said, laying back on the bed. She wore nothing but her panties and platform stripper heels, another man's cum all over her tits. "You better lock the door, Sweetie. I don't think you're going to want anyone to see the things I'm about to make you do."

He quickly obeyed, not bothering to argue about her being able to make him do anything she wanted. She smiled, realizing how deeply he'd accepted his place as her eager little bitch. He moved towards her, excited by the sight of her mostly naked body, tits glistening. As he reached the foot of the bed, Andrea once again squeezed her perfect little tits together with her biceps. "Come here," she commanded her pet. "Come lick all the cum off my tits."

He swallowed, eyes wide and nervous. "I'd rather…"

She interrupted him with a sharp sound like you might give a disobedient dog to shock it into compliance, then spoke. "I'd rather you stop being difficult and do what I asked without all the drama. We both know you're going to do it eventually. So, stop being a precious little princess and just do it now."

He nodded slightly and moved onto the bed. She laughed, spread her legs and opened her arms. He crawled between her legs. She wrapped her legs around her fully dressed boyfriend's waist, hooking her slutty heels behind his back like she might do with a man who was fucking her. Then she hugged her arms around him, palms pressing his back and his head, guiding his face down to her cum-smeared chest.

As much as he had tried to protest, he showed absolutely no hesitation as he began to lick and suck her semen caked tits.

"Mmmmm," Andrea purred. "Good boy."

She unhooked her legs from behind his back and slid one of her feet under him. She pressed her foot between his legs and felt his erection through his slacks. She moved her leg up and down, caressing his dick with her shin. "Such a hard little dick. We both know you love being my cum-eating little cleanup bitch."

He didn't say anything, but his eager tongue tickled her flesh as he lapped and suckled her sperm drenched tits. She pet his hair, rubbing her shin between his legs, purring with pleasure as he obediently served her. Tim worked his hips, trying to hump her leg, but she lightened the pressure, careful to just tease him without letting him get off yet. He continued to lick and suck her tits long after every drop of creamy sperm was sucked off her brown skin.

"I think my little cleanup bitch deserves a reward tonight," she said. She lifted her leg from between his legs and flicked the top button of his pants undone with her toe.

"Oh fuck," he said, quickly squirming out of his pants. "Oh shit, is this really happening?"

"Something is going to happen," she said with a laugh. "But probably not what you're expecting. Take off my panties."

He eagerly began to peel off her panties, leaving her naked except for her slutty heels. He knelt between her legs, naked and hard, looking at her with desperation, waiting for the permission she wasn't going to give him. Instead, she lifted both of her feet and pushed the heels into the soft flesh of his chest, making little dents. "Take off my shoes," she commanded.

His thin rod was throbbing as he carefully worked the fragile straps and buckles of her slutty heels one by one. She slid one foot out and he reverently took her shoe and set it carefully aside, before taking hold of her other foot letting her slip free of that shoe. Andrea sat up and kissed her boyfriend. One of his hands went to her hip, and the other to her soft, blonde hair. She took hold of the hand in her hair and squeezed it affectionately before pushing it down and placing it on his own erection. She held his hand, moving it back and forth, making him jerk himself.

She then stretched back, laying on her back, watching him jerk himself. She looked up at him smiling wickedly. He was kneeling between her feet, his erection in his hand, and she purred, "Keep stroking it. You can look at my pussy." She spread her legs wide, giving him a good view of her wet, recently fucked cunt. "I'm going to let you cum all over my little kitty tonight."

He was frantically stroking it, staring at her wet cunt, a little cum glistening on her pussy lips. "Please," he said. "Let me have sex with you. Please."

She laughed and raised one of her feet. "I've got something better for you to do. Something your much more suited to." She pressed her dainty foot to his face, the ball of her foot against his jaw, gently pushing his mouth open. With a graceful motion she turned and pointed her toes, pushing them into Tim's mouth.

Tim didn't hesitate to begin eagerly and obediently sucking her toes.

Andrea laughed, stretching out in a sexy pose for her boyfriend. She arched her back, showing off her wet tits as Tim sucked her toes one by one. He was staring at her glistening pussy, jerking himself as he pressed his tongue between her toes.

Andrea laughed, pulled her toes free of his lips and pressed the soul of her foot to his face. He began to shower it in slobber and affection, lapping at it with long strokes of his agile tongue.

"Mmmmm," Andrea purred. "Good boy. Do you think my feet are sexy?"

"Yes," he moaned. "Everything about you is sexy. You're so perfect. I love everything about you."

"My sweet little pet," Andrea purred. She moved one foot away from his face and offered him the other, pressing her toes into his mouth.

His tongue continued to dart between her toes, his fist pumping as he jacked himself.

"Please," he begged, voice muffled by her toes. "Please. Let me have sex with you."

Andrea laughed. "No. No sex for you until were married." She didn't know why she said that. She hadn't even considered marriage, and she never gave any thought to how long she'd torture Tim by withholding sex. But suddenly, Andrea felt like it was funny; putting such a distant condition on him ever getting to have sex, while she got fucked every single day. She laughed, rubbing her clit as he jerked over her, lapping at her foot like a pet.

"Tell me how much you love me," she said. "And thank me for letting you jack off over my pussy."

"I love you. I love you so much. Thank you. Thank you. Thank you."

"Good bitch," Andrea purred. "You are so lucky. You are such a lucky little pet."

"Thank you," Tim whimpered pumping his dick faster. He looked both pathetic and adorable and Andrea rubbed her clit faster, her body shivering with unexpected pleasure. "Hurry up," she said. "Hurry up and get yourself off. I still have lots of work for you to do."

As if just waiting for permission, Tim groaned and began to spurt hot jets of cum onto her pussy lips and the inside of her thigh. Her fingers got coated in his sperm as she continued to rub her hardened clit.

Andrea laughed, smearing his cum across her clit and smearing it across her pussy-lips. She could still feel the thick seed of the older man she had fucked just minutes before, swimming in her womb and dripping from her cunt.

Tim was panting from his orgasm, dick wilting in his hand as he slowly began to recover. Andrea kept rubbing herself. She moved her foot away from his mouth and gave him a playful, wet slap with it. She then hooked her foot behind his neck and began using it to pull him down.

"Okay," she purred as she sensed hesitation. "You had your fun. Now get back to work, Clean-up Bitch."

Tim looked for a moment at the mess he had just made. She was still rubbing her clit, cum on her hand, cum glistening on her pussy, cum dripping from her thighs. He swallowed with nervous anticipation, then bowed his head between her legs.

Andrea laughed as her obedient little pet began to lick the inside of her thighs, slurping up dripping globs of his own salty spunk as it dribbled down her smooth, brown flesh.

"Yes," Andrea purred. "Be a good boy. I know what's best for you."

He lapped one thigh then the other, swallowing down his own semen like an eager cum-slut.

"How's it taste?" Andrea asked. "Same as other guys?"

He didn't answer. Instead, having licked her thighs clean, he pressed his lips to her pussy and kissed her passionately. Andrea moaned, taking her cum splattered fingers from her clit, she ran them through Tim's hair. She moaned, arching her body and rubbing her pussy against his face as he kissed her cunt. His tongue began to wiggle inside her as he slurped up his cum, and the cum of another man mixed with her juices.

"Yes," Andrea moaned. "That's my bitch. That's my good little cleanup bitch."

Her body writhed as her boyfriend lapped up her juices, his face pressed hard against her cunt. She caressed his hair, smearing it with his own cum as she rocked against his face. He made hungry little noises as he ate her, slurping and sucking as he lapped at her wet flesh.

Before Tim, Andrea had never got off well from guys eating her. She wasn't sure if it was Tim's natural doting nature, his skillful little tongue, his obedience or just the filthiness of the situations she put him in, but every day she seemed to get off harder on his sweet little mouth. He had barely been down there five minutes, lapping, slurping, and sucking, her pussy smashing against his mouth as she humped his face, and already she was starting to feel the electric shivers of orgasm tingling inside her.

She tightened her grip in his hair. "Yes bitch," she moaned. "Oh, fuck yes. My good little bitch. My obedient little man. I love my pet. I love my little cleanup bitch!"

His voice was muffled by wet flesh as he cried back, "I love you too."

Andrea laughed, twisting her grip in his hair as her ecstasy built. She hadn't meant to profess love for Tim, but she supposed it was true. She did love him. She did love her obedient little cuckold slave. "Shut up," she commanded. "Focus. I'm so close. I'm so fucking close."

His tongue began to work faster, the suction of his mouth increasing, the sound of his filthy work filling the room. His hands lovingly caressed her flesh as his mouth devoured her juices.

"Yes," she cried. "Fuck yes. Good bitch. Good little bitch."

Her body began to spasm as her orgasm took over.

Andrea's upper body lifted, using her grip on his hair for leverage as she pulled his face harder into her cunt. She felt throbbing moving threw her body as she shivered with electric pleasure. She let out a little squeal, her thighs tightening on the sides of her boyfriend's face, smothering him with hot, wet, cum-drenched pussy as she lost herself in blissful release.

Finally, the ecstasy passed, and she collapsed back to the mattress with a deep, satisfied sigh. Her body relaxed and her thighs released their iron grip on Tim's moisture glistened face. Tim began panting for much needed, and well-earned oxygen. Andrea pressed the ball of her spit-wet foot to his forehead and pushed him away from her so she could roll over.

Andrea turned on her side, so relaxed she could have drifted off to sleep in the strange, cum-stained bed.

Tim cuddled up behind her, spooning her and gently kissing one of her small, brown shoulders. "I love you too," he said again.

Andrea laughed. "I said it. Now stop gloating." She could feel Tim, his dick already hard again, throbbing against her ass. "You're still not getting your little dick wet until you put a ring on this finger." She held up one hand waving it in the air as if to demonstrate where the ring would go. She felt excited and proud of herself, for finding a new way to deny him sex, perhaps indefinitely.

They cuddled on the strange bed for a while, then finally Andrea started to rise. She gave her boyfriend an affectionate hair tussle. "Get dressed and take me home," she said. "We can watch a little tv, then I'll let you draw me a bath and give me a massage."

Tim practically jumped out of bed, eager to serve.

Her Cuckold Valentine

Andrea giggled as she led the tall, powerfully built stud through the door. The gorgeous young man had no idea he was part of a special Valentine's Night surprise for Tim. "My boyfriend's not here," she said loud enough for her little pet to hear. "So, we can fuck in every room of his house."

The stud lifted her off her feet and pressed her against the wall. They began kissing frantically, her soft body smashed between the hallway wall and the young stud's unyielding frame. She wrapped her legs around his long, lean torso, writhing against him, her long, slender body pinned.

She couldn't hear her boyfriend, but she knew Tim was home. She had told him to be home, and he always obeyed. He didn't know why he had to be home, or anything about the show she was about to give him, but he was there.

Perhaps this would all be easier if her boyfriend wasn't so nervous and ashamed of what he was. Then she wouldn't have to lie to this guy. Her and her sweet little boyfriend could just find some guy who was into being watched. But Tim could barely admit he wanted to watch, even to himself. If some other guy knew, poor little Tim would curl up in shame. It was much easier just to pretend she was cheating. Plus, the young stud she was with now (she thought Kevin was his name) loved banging cheating sluts. The powerful young man might even be creeped out if he knew that her boyfriend secretly wanted to watch it as much as she needed to get it.

She had passed on a shift on Valentine's night at the strip club, even though it was a fantastic night for tips, just to give her doting little boyfriend his first chance to actually watch.

All Tim needed to do, was to have the sense to hide, and to stay quiet.

"Fuck," she moaned, again, loud enough for her boyfriend to hear wherever he was hiding. "Carry me down the hall, to the living room. I want you to fuck me on the couch."

The man pulled her from the wall, his strong hands supporting her by the ass and the small of her back as she continued to wiggle against his solid and unyielding frame. She began kissing and nibbling at the man's thick neck as he carried her down the hall and into the living room. She glanced around, looking for signs of her pet. She could smell delicious food, and looking over her lover's shoulder, she saw the dinning table set up perfectly in the next room; candles lit, and dishes carefully laid like a fancy restaurant. It looked like she wasn't the only one planning a Valentine's Night surprise. She was happy. She couldn't imagine anything better than a romantic dinner with her doting pet, after a good, hard fucking from another man.

Andrea continued to look around as the man carried her to the couch. She caught a hint of movement out of the corner of her eye and glanced over to see the bedroom door, just slightly move. She stared into the dark slit of the slightly open doorway and saw dim movement there. Tim had chosen the perfect spot to hide and watch the action. As the man held Andrea over the couch, she smiled over his shoulder at the ajar doorway, winked and blew her pet a teasing kiss.

She was awakened back to the moment and the presence of the hot young stud as he pushed her off him, sending her spilling onto the couch. The man pulled off his shirt and exposed his lean, cut muscles. Andrea bit her lower lip, quivering at the delicious sight of the man's athletic build. She slithered out of her dress. She wasn't wearing a bra, and sat sprawled on the couch in nothing but a slutty thong, and even sluttier platform heels.

She watched as Kevin began to undo his jeans, then slide them down. She had felt the young stud's massive dick, but it was even bigger than she realized, and it looked delicious, pressed against the cotton of his tight-fitting boxer briefs.

"Oh," Andrea moaned, looking at her lover but directing her statement to her boyfriend, hiding in the sliver of darkness behind cracked open bedroom door. "Your dick is so fucking big."

Kevin teasingly pulled down his underwear just enough to expose half of his huge, throbbing, vein-crossed shaft. He looked from her face to his own massive cock with an arrogant smile. "A little bigger than your boyfriend?"

Andrea laughed and held up her hand where both her boyfriend and her lover could see. She made a sign with her fingers, the universal sign for a little dick. "My boyfriend isn't even in your league," she said. She placed her other hand on one of her small, perky breasts, squeezing it as she felt herself getting hotter and wetter.

The man still stared proudly at his own monstrous erection, as impressed with it as she was. He looked back at her face. "So why you date him if he's such a little dick loser?"

Andrea gave the man a wicked smile. "Because he's my little dick loser. Every girl should own one."

The man laughed. "Damn you're a filthy slut. Open up. Let's put that dirty mouth to work."

Andrea slipped off the couch, and squatted on her massive heels, she reached up and took hold of the stud's underwear and began peeling it the rest of the way down. He held his dick at the base, playfully smacking it against her face. Andrea turned her face side to side, letting him slap her cheeks with his beautifully engorged rod, then she pursed her lips at let it slap against her mouth. The slaps of his hot, hard cock felt exhilaratingly solid, like warning taps with a deadly baton. Finally, he lowered his throbbing meat level with her glossy red lips and waited.

She placed both her hands on the man's strong ass, opened her mouth wide and dipped her head forward, while pulling him towards her, filling her mouth with thick, delicious cock.

The man moaned with rewarding pleasure as she began to slide her glossy lips up and down his thick, rippled dong. He rolled slightly back on his heels. "Fuck," he said. "Your boyfriend may have a little dick, but you're no stranger to sucking big ones."

She looked up at him, trying to give him innocent eyes, batting her eyelashes as she slid her mouth up and down his throbbing tool. The stud was swaying, enjoying the work of her wet mouth and skillful tongue. She tasted musky precum and savored the flavor for a moment before sliding him out of her mouth. She looked at the doorway and gave her hiding boyfriend a wink before she said, "Let's take this to the bedroom. I want you to fuck me on my bed."

She held her stud by the base of his cock now, teasing the tip of his dick with her tongue while looking up at him, waiting for his answer. From the other room she could barely here the soft shish of quiet movement as her man scrambled for another hiding place, knowing he was about to be closer to the action. Andrea giggled to help cover the sound, and started slapping herself with the thick, now wet cock.

Kevin smiled down at her, enjoying watching her slap herself with his magnificent cock. "Lead the way," he finally said, obviously not caring where he fucked the slinky blonde.

Andrea stood up, keeping hold of the stud's dick, and gently pulled him behind her, swaying as she led him slowly towards the bedroom. As she entered the room, she flipped on the lights so her boyfriend could have good light for the show. She glanced around as she led the stud into the room by his cock. Tim was well hidden, but she thought she knew where he was.

The closet door was closed, but it had an old-fashioned keyhole; the kind someone could look through. She let go of her lover's dick and turned around, pressing her body against him. "Wait for me on the bed," she purred, then kissed the stud, driving her tongue into his mouth for just a moment. "I'll be right there."

He moved onto the bed, stripping off what was left of his clothes as he did. Andrea walked up to the closet door and pulled it open just enough to access it, but not enough to show the young stud what was hiding inside.

Sure enough, Tim was crouched on the closet floor, surrounded by dozens of slutty high heel shoes. He was still wearing his shirt, a salmon button down she had picked out for him, but he had no slacks, his lower half completely naked. His little erection was clutched in one hand. He looked up at her guiltily, like a puppy who had just gotten in the trash.

Andrea leaned into the closet and kissed him on the lips. She then unbuckled her slutty platform heels and kicked them one by one into the closet, hitting her boyfriend with an amusing "Thunk." She then peeled off her panties, wet with her juices, and threw them into Tim's face. Tim snatched the panties and held them to his face, breathing them in. Andrea closed the closet door and began swaying back to her lover, waiting on the bed, massive dick throbbing as it pointed at the ceiling.

Andrea noticed for the first time, a trail of rose petals leading from the foot of the bed to the dresser. The trail of red petals led all the way to a little jewelry box sitting in the middle of the dresser. She smiled. A Valentine's present. Her boyfriend was so considerate. She was going to be sure and reward him, after she was done getting fucked by a real man's big, beautiful cock.

Andrea crawled onto the bed, moving like a cat as she squirmed up Kevin's hairy, muscular legs. She moved up and kissed Kevin on the mouth, rubbing her body against his, her pussy flooding with wet heat. She straddled the hot young stud and was about to lower herself onto his cock, when she decided to turn around. She switched to a reverse cowgirl position so she could face the closet door.

The stud put one of his big hands on the generous curve from her tiny waist to her hip. His other hand caressed her long, narrow back, fingers passing over the tribal ink of her tramp-stamp.

Andrea bit her lower lip and stared at her boyfriend's keyhole as she slowly lowered herself down onto Kevin's enormous prick. She leaned forward and braced her hands on Kevin's thighs, using her biceps to squeeze her tits together as her cunt began to engulf the stud's mushroom head. She whimpered, lowering herself more, staring at the keyhole as she felt the throbbing heat of the powerful stud begin to pulse inside her.

"Yes," she purred as she descended the final inches and felt his pulse thundering deep inside her. "Oh yes. You have such a big dick. Such a big, perfect cock."

The man slapped her hard on her ass. "Tell me how much bigger I am then your pussy boyfriend."

"Yes," she cried, the slap making her pussy flood even more. She stared at the keyhole, imagining Tim staring back, his dick in one hand and her panties in the other. "Yes," she whimpered. "You're so much bigger than my little, pussy boyfriend. I love it. I love your bigger, better cock."

He slapped her ass again, her little rump turning red and jiggling slightly as she moaned with pleasure.

"Tell me how much you like fucking me."

Andrea purred, rocking forward and back on the man's lap, grinding his fat cock deep inside her hot, wet cunt. "I love getting fucked by you," she cried. "I love cheating on my pussy boyfriend with such a big stud, with such a superior cock."

Andrea rid him slow, staring at the keyhole, her body writhing, her face full of pleasure. She whimpered as she rocked and grinded on the massive, throbbing cock. She knew Tim would be jerking it in that closet. She could feel his eyes on her from across the room. "Fuck yes," she whimpered, riding Kevin as his big hands moved across her sides and over her ass. "Oh, fuck yes. I love it. I love your big, hard cock."

One of the man's hands tightened firmly on her hip, as the other slid up her back and twisted itself into her mane of lustrous blonde hair. He began to take control of her, firmly pulling her hair, as his fingers tightened into the flesh of her waist. He began to pump into her, fucking her from below with expert control of both his body and hers.

"Yes," she cried. "Yes. Fuck me hard. Fuck me hard right in the bed I share with my boyfriend." She stared at her boyfriend's keyhole, as she whimpered with pain and pleasure.

But her eyes kept drifting over to that tail of roses and the small jewelry box. Earrings? The box was small, but she bet it was expensive. She felt tingles of excitement for her gift, even as she felt tingles of pleasure moving in her core.

"Fuck me," she whimpered. "Fuck me hard with your big dick. Yes. Oh, fuck yes." She bounced against her stud, learning his timing, their bodies slamming harder and harder together.

The smell of sex filled the room as did the sound of their bodies slapping together. The sound of Andrea's whimpers, and Kevin's moans grew louder and louder as they fucked harder and faster. Andrea's body began to pulse with ecstasy. Her mind grew blank except the awareness of hot, pulsating cock, the thought of her boyfriend watching, and the excitement for her gift on the dresser. Her body began to twitch and spasm as her nervous system began to short circuit with powerful orgasm.

She cried out, her body writhing and twitching in bliss as Kevin continued to plow her from below. "Oh fuck!" she cried. "Your dick! Your beautiful, amazing dick! I love it! I love your big fucking dick!" She thrashed and whimpered, grabbing her own tits and squeezing as orgasm cascaded through her slender, curving frame. Finally, she collapsed forward, his big cock still throbbing inside her. She hugged his legs, kissing his knees. "Oh fuck," she whimpered as she slowly recovered. She began to slowly grind against him again, her pussy sensitive and throbbing. "Oh shit. You're still so fucking hard. Oh fuck. I want you to cum baby. I want you to cum inside me."

"I want to cum in that dirty, cheating mouth of yours. I want him to taste me next time you kiss."

"Mmmmm," Andrea purred. She wanted that cum in her mouth, but she couldn't stop thinking about her new jewelry. The anticipation was making her crazy. "I would love to eat your cum, baby. But first, I have to know what my Sweetie bought me."

Kevin followed her gaze to the romantic gesture waiting on the dresser and he laughed. "By all means," he said. "Open it. I'm curious how much this guy loves the dirty little slut who's begging for my cum."

Andrea laughed with giddy excitement, hoped off the man's hard cock and hurried over to the dresser. Her lover followed her, his big dick glistening with juices as it pointed firmly at the ceiling. Andrea snapped up the jewelry box and threw it open.

"Oh fuck," she gasped in shock. Behind her, she could hear Kevin laughing. She was staring down at the perfect diamond of a beautiful engagement ring. She felt dizzy with giddy joy. She had no idea. She hadn't seriously thought about marrying her little pet. Bringing up marriage had just been another way to tease him. She never imagined he would go through with it.

Behind her, the stud was laughing. "Are you going to say yes?"

Andrea didn't have to answer, when she turned and the man saw the glowing smile on her face, he laughed even harder. "The poor little guy has no idea what a hot, cheating slut he's about to marry."

Andrea wanted to proudly announce that her sweet little man loved the cheating slut in her as much as the rest of her, but she knew Tim was still shy. He wouldn't want this powerful man to know what an obedient little bitch he was, so she just shrugged and glanced at the keyhole. "Secrets are fun," she said. She took out the ring and it dazzled in the light. She slipped it on her finger and held up her hand looking at the diamond shine.

She noticed her lover was looking at her with a wicked thrill in his eyes, glancing at the expensive ring. His big dick, slippery with her juices, was still so deliciously hard. "Come here," the man said. "Come celebrate your coming engagement by sucking a real man's cock."

Andrea stuck her tongue out teasingly, then darted away from Kevin, as if she was going to make him chase her, but she stopped directly in front of the closet Tim hid in. She dropped to her knees a few paces from the keyhole, where Tim would have a perfect view. Andrea held out her left hand, diamond sparkling, and gestured the stud towards her.

He walked up and stopped right in front of her, his powerful frame towering over her as she knelt on the floor. She knew, on the other side of that closet door, just an arms reach away, her boyfriend was stroking himself as he watched. She gazed up at her lover and smiled, then she turned her face to the perfect angle and gazed at the keyhole.

She reached up with her left hand, freshly ringed finger on display as she took hold of his pussy-wet meat. She gazed into the dark slit of the keyhole, making sure her new diamond was visible as she stroked her stud.

"I can't wait to do this as a married woman," she said, stroking her lover but speaking to her boyfriend. Her hand slid back and forth, feeling her lover throb powerfully in her hand. "I'm going to suck so many big, hard cocks when I'm a lawfully wedded wife."

Her lover laughed. "You are a dirty little freak," he said.

She looked up at him and gave him a wicked smile and a wink as she licked the head of his pulsating cock, tasting her own pussy on his tip. She looked back at the keyhole, smiling lovingly as she took the man's cock between her glossy red lips.

The man moaned, already close to orgasm from all the fucking. "Oh yes, suck that cock. Suck that cock, you dirty little slut. Kneel in the room you share with your pussy boyfriend and suck a real man's cock."

Andrea continued staring at the keyhole, feeling her pussy boyfriend's complete attention as she bobbed her head, driving the stud's massive cock into her mouth and down her throat, her hand still stroking his fat shaft.

"Yes," Kevin moaned, hand in her blonde hair, beginning to hump her face. He rocked back and forth, fucking her face and her fist as she pumped and sucked him, diamond engagement ring glistening. Andrea slurped and slobbered as her head bobbed and her fist pumped, Kevin face-fucking her as her boyfriend peeped through the keyhole.

"Yes," Kevin groaned. "Oh, fuck yes. Make me cum. Make me cum, then kiss your little pussy boyfriend with your filthy whore mouth." His body began to spasm as he exploded into her mouth.

She gulped down his cream even as he held her head and began to pull out. Hot jizz shot across her lips and face, squirting across her skin. He jerked himself free of her grip and began pumping himself, shooting hot cream across her hand, drenching her diamond ring. After claiming her ring with his hot, sticky jizz, he shoved himself back between her cum-splattered lips and finished emptying his balls.

"Oh, fuck yes," he sighed with satisfaction, as he pulled himself back out of her mouth. He looked down on her on her knees beneath him, cum streaked across her face and painted across her wedding ring. He laughed. "That was fucking hot. I need a fucking drink. You got anything strong?" he asked.

She swallowed most of the musky sperm that filled her mouth so she could speak. "There's some good whiskey in the cabinet by the fridge. Pour me one too?"

He pat her on the head and walked away.

She watched the man leave the room, and when he left, she opened the closet door. Her boyfriend was still kneeling on the carpet, but his dick was soft, her panties balled up in his hand, turned into a makeshift cumrag.

She leaned into the closet and kissed him, her sperm covered tongue pressing between Tim's lips and wiggling in his mouth. She spit some sticky wads of cream from her mouth to his, then pulled away, smiling happily. "Yes," she said. "I accept. No longer my pussy-boyfriend. Soon to be my pussy fiancé." She giggled and he blushed.

She held out her hand, displaying her cum-caked ring as if showing off her diamond to a girlfriend, but Tim understood the silent command. He bowed his head forward and began to lick the stud's cum off the diamond ring. His tongue moved across her skin, and between her finger, cleaning her. She then leaned forward and let her fiancé lick the semen from her face.

She kissed Tim again than said, "I'm probably going to let that guy fuck me a few more times before he goes. So, you just wait in here and stay quiet as a mouse." She then took her cum filled panties out of his hand. She used her other hand to pinch Tim's chin and pull his mouth open. She then gave him a wicked smile and stuffed the makeshift cum-rag into his mouth. "Quiet as a mouse," she reminded him as she muzzled him in cum-soaked lace. She kissed his forehead affectionately, then stood up and picked out a little silk robe, slipped it on and closed the closet door. She blew the keyhole a kiss then went out towards the kitchen to share a drink with her stud.

Romantic Cuckold Date Night

Andrea looked across the table at her adorable fiancé. He looked very clean and nice, all dressed up in his suit. She wore a clinging red dress, a long slit up the side adding a slutty flair to the otherwise simple but elegant gown.

"This place is so expensive," Tim whispered. "Are you sure you don't want me to pay?"

"That's so sweet, but tonight I want to take care of my sweet little bitch. I made such good tips last night my pet deserves to get spoiled too."

"Thank you," he said shyly. "Did you… how was work last night? You never really said."

Andrea laughed. She knew what her nervous little pet wanted to hear. He loved all the filthy details of her slutty adventures. "I got fucked really hard by one of my regulars. He took me into VIP and fucked my every hole with his huge cock. I came so many times I lost count. He came so much in my cunt, I was dripping with sperm. Didn't you taste it last night?"

Tim just blushed, so adorably shy when she talked about what a filthy little cum gobbler he was.

"Of course you tasted it. Anyway, I almost came again when he handed me that fat roll of money. I guess he just landed a big sale or something and was feeling generous. He told me to buy my fiancé something nice with it. He was kidding, but I thought, you know what, I should get my pet something nice. What is nicer than treating my pet to a romantic dinner with that fat roll of fuck-money? So, I went straight to tell my boss I wasn't going to work tonight. He asked why and I told him it was so I could have a romantic evening with my fiancé. Of course, it was late notice, so he made me blow him. He came so much, squirting all over my face and tits, it was such a filthy mess." Andrea's nipples hardened remembering all that hot spunk squirting in streaks across her face and tits. "I've told you how delicious my boss's sperm is. I was in heaven, licking that filthy jizz off my own tits and rubbing cream into my soft skin."

Tim squirmed, frustrated and aroused, an erection throbbing in his slacks. Andrea laughed at her pet. "Sorry. Didn't mean to get you all worked up before dinner." Andrea looked at her needy little pet, laughing at his desperation, but she realized, she had gotten herself pretty worked up too. "Tell you what," she told her fiancé. "Why don't you go off to the bathroom and spank your little monkey. I'm going to go find that handsome waiter of ours and see if he'll spank me."

Tim swallowed hard and hesitated. Was he still trying to pretend he didn't want her to fuck every hot, alpha stud she came across, or was he actually conflicted? Andrea laughed. It didn't matter. "Suit yourself," she purred. "Jack off or don't. But I'm going to go get some good dick either way." She leaned forward, kissed her fiancé's cheek and gave him a flirty little wave as she slithered off in her slinky red dress.

Andrea headed back towards the kitchen until she found her waiter. He was in his early twenties, tall and lean, with vibrant, youthful skin and lush black hair. He had disarming grey eyes and a confident, cold smile that gave him a slightly cruel look.

As she approached him, he frowned slightly. "Is something wrong, ma'am?" he said.

She almost laughed. His manners were forced. His eyes looked like he was trying to decide between slapping her stupid or fucking the shit out of her. Besides, they were too close in age for him to be calling her ma'am, especially in this slutty dress. She moved closer, almost pressing against him, whispering so only he could hear. "Yes. Something's wrong. My fiancé has a little dick."

The waiter didn't show any sign of shock or amusement. He just said, "Yeah. I got that vibe from him."

"I got all dressed up," she purred. "It would be a shame to waste it all just on him." Andrea knew guys like this loved to hear the competition belittled, even though Tim was clearly no competition. "I need to feel a real man inside me tonight. Is there somewhere we can go for a few minutes?"

"Follow me," he said. He still seemed calm and professional as he led her through dinning room to a hallway.

Andrea glanced at her table and saw that Tim had slunk off to do his nasty business. "Good boy," she thought, strangely proud of her well-trained pet.

"There's a storeroom back here," the waiter said as they slipped into the hallway. "The door locks so we can..."

Andrea noticed the door to the men's room on their left. "I've got a better idea," she purred. She grabbed the waiter by the wrist and began tugging him toward the door. "How hot would it be to fuck me stupid on the filthy men's room floor?"

For the first time, her waiter showed a reaction. He shook his head, but smiled, "You are a little freak, aren't you? It's not enough to cheat, you've got to do it as nasty as possible, don't you?"

Andrea nodded, smiling wickedly, pulling the hot stud towards the men's room door. He stopped her and suddenly pounded on the door. "Anyone in there!" he yelled.

The power and authority in the man's voice made Andrea's tummy quiver. She was sure her little bitch, if he was in there, would have an even stronger reaction. Without Tim even knowing what it was about, she was sure that just the sound of that deep, commanding voice would make her fiancé too terrified to squeak.

When no answer was returned, the waiter pushed Andrea into the men's room. The waiter moved in, ignoring her for a moment as he opened a supply closet. Andrea looked around. She could see her pet's shoes underneath one of the stalls. She moved toward him. The waiter pulled out an "Out of Service" sign and hung it on the outside of the men's room door, as she slid closer to the stall and whispered. "Spank it quiet, Sweetie, and enjoy the show."

Tim's feet pulled up out of view with a quiet rustle as the waiter closed the men's room door and bolted it. The waiter looked at her, seeing her at the other side of the bathroom. "Filthy enough for you?"

The bathroom was actually very clean, but she nodded. She walked to a sink directly across from her pet's stall, her tall, slutty heels clicking on the tile. She wiggled her body, pulling up her tight dress until the slit rose to her waist, then she slipped her panties down. She pulled her panties off, then flung them away, letting them fly into her fiancé's stall. Andrea slithered onto the edge of the sink, and parted her legs, waiting.

The waiter moved up, pressing against her as she sat on the sink. His hands groping, the waiter began to kiss her. She kissed him back passionately, her hands feeling the solid muscles of his back as her feet caressed the back of his legs through his black uniform slacks. Her dress still pulled up, she could feel his bulge, massive and throbbing, against her bare cunt, her juices coating the crotch of his slacks.

Andrea wanted that cock inside her, but she wanted her pet to get a good look at the massive treat she was about to get, so she pushed the waiter back and slithered off the sink, dropping to her knees on the bathroom tile. She caressed his bulge through his slacks, looking up at him, smiling hungrily. Her cunt was tingling with electricity at the thought of this beautiful cock throbbing inside her. She gazed up at him as she kissed his wet bulge. She kept eye-contact as she bit her lower lip and began to undo the waiter's belt. She slipped his slacks and boxers down to his ancles, rubbing her face and hair against his massive erection. She leaned back on her heels and took a good look at it. It was beautiful; long and slightly curved, thick and bulging with contours and veins. She began to gently caress it and kissed the tip. She gazed up at the powerful young man, still maintaining eye contact, keeping the focus on her so he wouldn't be looking around as she stroked him.

"Look at this big, gorgeous cock," she said, looking at the waiter but talking to her pet. The waiter just stared down at her, his grey eyes calm and unflinching, showing nothing of what he felt, but his throbbing erection giving away his hunger. She kissed the tip again, giving it a flick with her tongue. She let a little spit wash across her tongue and lapped it around that swollen, purple cockhead. She kissed the tip again, now dripping with saliva. As she leaned back, a long dribble of drool was dropping from his tip. It was glistening in the bright washroom lights as it ran down from his tip towards her brown knees. She caught the drool in her free hand and smeared it across the man's big, hairy balls, caressing him. Out of the corner of her eyes, she could see her fiancé peering cautiously over the top of the stall, standing on the toilet seat.

Andrea purred, stroking the waiter's shaft gently, caressing his balls wetly, "I'm going to cum so hard on this big, powerful cock. I want it slamming inside me. I want it raw. I want this cock to explode inside me. I want to go back to my date filled with hot, sticky jizz." Andrea kissed the head of the cock once more.

The waiter showed no reaction, but his hand took her by the chin and guided her to her feet. He kissed her again, his tongue plunging into her mouth as her fiancé watched from the side. Andrea grabbed her dress and pulled it up over her head, casting it aside. Now she stood, completely naked except of her stiletto heels and a heart-shaped locket that Tim had given her, dangling between her perky young tits. The waiter took hold of her, his big, strong hands gripping her hips. He lifted her up and set her back on the edge of the sink. Andrea spread her legs, hooked her heels behind the waiter's thighs, and used them to pull him towards her.

"Fuck me," she purred. "Fuck me with that big, amazing cock."

She kissed the waiter, wrapping her legs around him, her ass on the edge of the sink, the heat of his fat cock pressing against her. She worked her hips, grinding against him, whimpering as their tongues wrestled back and forth between their hot, wet mouths. One of her hands reached under the back of his shirt, feeling his muscles as her other hand squeezed his strong ass. He reached between them and guided his engorged prick to her wet opening. They continued kissing as he rocked his hips forward and pushed his thick tool inside her hungry, quivering cunt. Andrea moaned and threw her head back, her blonde hair trailing down her back towards the sink as she was overwhelmed with the sensation of throbbing heat filling her womb.

"Yes," she whimpered. "Fuck me. Fuck me."

The waiter began to press back and forth inside her. She could see her fiancé peeking over the top of the stall door, terrified of being caught. She moved her hands from behind the waiter and reached up, interlacing her fingers behind the man's head as she leaned back even more. She braced her shoulders against the cold tile as she pulled the waiters face to her chest. She buried his face in her tits, holding him there as he kissed and sucked her hard pink nipples.

"Yes," she whimpered. "Suck my tits. Don't stop. Don't stop. Suck them while you fuck me. I love it so much. Don't stop."

The waiter rocked back and forth, pumping his steel-like rod inside her, his face buried in her tits. She looked at her fiancé. He was more confident now, looking over the stall, staring at her as she got fucked. He was swaying slightly, obviously pumping his little hard-on behind the stall. She made eye contact with her pet, letting him see the pleasure on her face as she got fucked.

"Yes," Andrea moaned, staring into Tim's eyes. "Oh yes. Your dick is so big. I love your big, hard cock."

The waiter was grunting, fucking her harder with each thrust, not caring about anything but getting off on her on her tight little body. She writhed against him, his big prick making her shudder with pleasure every time he pumped it deep inside her. She stared into Tim's eyes and licked her lips, wet pink tongue passing over her glossy red lips. Waves of delicious pleasure moved through her and registered in her passion-filled expressions. She mouthed silently to her pet, "I love you, Bitch."

He mouthed back, "I love you," pumping his little dick frantically out of view.

Andrea continued to stare at her pet, writhing and moaning as the contours of thick, throbbing cock pressed through the soft flesh lining her hot, wet cunt.

"Yes," Andrea whimpered, moaning with more and more pleasure, the waiter's face buried in her tits as he nibbled and sucked her nipples. "Oh, fuck yes. I love this big hard cock. I love getting fucked by this beautiful cock."

The waiter grunted, probably not even listening to her words as he smashed his cock inside her with growing intensity.

The smell of sex filled the air as the sounds of whimpering, grunting and bodies slapping together echoed from the walls. Tim was pumping away at his little dick, swaying side to side as he watched her get fucked by a stronger, more powerful man. Tim's eyes were full of frustrated pleasure, desperate devotion, and total worshipful obedience as he stared into Andrea's face. Andrea stared back, letting her pet see the pleasure in her expression as she inched closer and closer to orgasm with every rough, indifferent thrust from the powerful stud that was using her tight, young body.

"Yes," Andrea whimpered, her body rocking against the waiter's solid frame. She kept eye contact with her fiancé, moaning and watching his expression as he jacked himself. "Oh, fuck yes. Fuck me hard. Fuck me like a dirty whore with your big, hard cock."

She could see her pet's head bobbing as he jacked himself harder, matching the pace of the stud that was pounding her cunt. She felt dizzy with tingles, her body shuddering with every thrust. She stared at her slave over her lover's head, as her lover sucked her tits. She let Tim see the pleasure in her face as she watched the thrill and desperate pleasure in his.

"Yes," she whimpered for both of them. "Fuck me. Fuck me hard. Fuck me with that gorgeous cock. Fuck me!" Her voice was growing higher and more shrill as hard cock throbbed and pounded deep in her womb and her fiancé jerked his dick frantically.

Andrea wanted to close her eyes as the pulse of orgasm neared, but she kept her eyes open, gazing into her pet's eyes as the intensity built and built. Suddenly she cried out, her face lighting up with blissful ecstasy as her body convulsed with sensory overload. She could see the look of recognition in her fiancé's face as he realized what he was watching, then he too began to orgasm, spurting cum on the side of the stall, probably smearing the graffiti that someone had written in marker.

Andrea's body convulsed against the waiter as he continued pounding her hard, grunting.

"Oh fuck," the waiter suddenly groaned as her pleasure-filled cunt spasmed around his meat. "Oh, fuck yes!"

"Cum in my pussy!" Andrea cried, her body still exploding with orgasm. "Fill me up with cum and send me back to my sweet little man." Her sweet little man was leaning against the stall of the door, exhausted and panting, squeezing out the last drops of his sperm. Andrea's orgasm continued to linger, her body shivering and her mind spinning.

"Fuck yes," the waiter grunted. "Fuck yes. Take it. Take it home to your little bitch."

And suddenly the waiter began to explode inside her with incredible power. Her orgasm stopped fading and began to intensify, her body jerking with each thrust and each blast of hot cum into her womb. The waiter came and came and then kept cumming. She shivered and moaned as the intensity of her orgasm built to a second explosion of ecstasy. Finally, she felt the waiters face pull away from her drool covered tits, and his big dick slide out from her slippery, sperm-filled cunt.

She smiled, sweaty and dizzy and buzzing with satisfaction.

The waiter pulled up his slacks and looked in the mirror to fix his uniform. Andrea glanced to the stall to verify her pet was hiding once more.

"That was amazing," she moaned.

The stone-face waiter smiled disarmingly. "I hope you didn't cost me my job. You were loud as fuck."

Andrea smiled back as she slipped off the sink and looked for her dress. "If you do get fired, I think I could talk my fiancé into hiring me a yoga instructor."

The waiter laughed as he went to the door, unlocked it and peered outside. He pulled the sign off the door and threw it aside before slipping out into the hallway. Andrea slipped out a moment behind him. No one gave her a second look, aside from the usual appreciative glances and the lingering stares at her ass as she slithered back to her table, sat down and finished her glass of wine.

A few minutes later, Tim began walking sheepishly back from the men's room. Tim shuffled quietly back to the table. Now that the passion had passed, he seemed ashamed. They had spent the bulk of the time she was getting fucked gazing into each other's eyes, but now he couldn't bring himself to make eye contact. His face was red with embarrassment as he slid his chair back up to the table. The appetizers had arrived, and Andrea smeared her finger across the skin of one of the shrimp, coating the tip with garlic butter. She brought her finger to her lips and tasted the sauce, eyeing her pet as he sheepishly looked down.

"That was so romantic," she said dreamily.

He looked at her with surprise and skepticism.

She gave him a flirty smile. "The fact that you love and trust me enough to watch me get fucked by a real man. The fact that you're willing to show that weak, pathetic, perverted part of yourself to me. That's selfless devotion, pet. I'm proud of you."

He lit up with joy, then started to speak with a hint of hopeful excitement, "When am I going to get to…"

Knowing the question, she interrupted him with another gentle reminder, "No sex for you till marriage sweetie. Good boys wait for it, right?" She studied his face, still sucking her finger.

He nodded, only a hint of disappointment and resignation in his voice. "Right," he agreed.

"In the meantime," she purred. "That fucking stud of a waiter came so hard in me. I think those big balls of his held a gallon of filthy sperm. Why don't you crawl under the table and have a taste?" She smiled wickedly and gave him a sexy wink.

Tim looked around to see if anyone was watching then slipped under the tablecloth. Beneath the table, he began crawling across the floor, hidden by the long, draping tablecloth. Andrea scooted her chair closer, adjusted the tablecloth to conceal her lap, and spread her legs. She felt her pet settle between her slim brown thighs, his soft hair and smooth face tickling her flesh. She sighed happily as her obedient pet began to lap quietly at her freshly fucked pussy.

She savored the sensation of her hungry slave lapping at her as the waiter came with more wine.

"Your fiancé step out?" he asked as he refilled her glass with red.

"I sent him on an errand," she purred. "I see you still have a job after all."

The waiter shrugged with a boyish smile. "I was being dramatic. My boss would probably give me a high five if he knew, as long as your boyfriend doesn't find out and complain."

Andrea bit her lower lip, feeling a quiver of pleasure as her fiancé slurped silently between her legs, lapping up the waiter's potent seed. "I don't think my pet is going to complain," she purred.

Bridal Shower Humiliation

Andrea looked around the room. Her little bridal shower looked more like schoolboy's fantasy. All her girlfriends were strippers, and they sat around the room looking hot and lustrous. They were dressed casually, but even their casual clothes looked slutty and enticing. Most of them wore their workout clothes, coming to or from the gym on this Sunday afternoon. In their yoga pants or sweat-shorts, summer dresses or faded denim cutoff shorts they looked as exciting and delicious as if they were dressed to the nines. Andrea was slimly built, but most of her friends had big artificial breasts that stood out from their tight, athletic frames.

Andrea wasn't necessarily into girls, but most of her friends were. She had let several of these girls go down in her in the past, before she had met Tim, her perfect little pussy-eater. Andrea picked up another present. Around her were assorted the presents she'd already opened: dildo's, vibrators and anal beads. In polite society everyone would have to pretend these were all gag gifts, but the girls in this room knew that all these toys would be getting used, one way or the other.

Andrea pulled the ribbon on the small box and opened it. "What's that?" she asked, staring down at the small, pink, plastic device. She held the little thing up for everyone to see.

Kim laughed. The Asian doll's big, fake tits looked like they'd pop out of her black sports-bra top, her slinky Asian hips and tight ass hugged by the fabric of her black yoga pants. She spoke in a purring voice, her accent a mix between Korean and British. "That is a chastity device, for your soon-to-be husband. You lock his dick in it. I had to guess on the size. Extra, extra small, right?"

Andrea looked at it again, then laughed when she finally understood how to use it. It was a little pink cage, just big enough to close around a small, limp penis and prevent it from getting hard. The hard plastic material was wrapped in a slightly soft, somewhat squishy rubberized shell. There was a tiny little padlock to lock it closed. "Oh my," Andrea laughed, "doesn't it hurt?"

Kim shrugged as if it had never even occurred to her to worry about such a thing. "You keep saying how sweet and well-behaved he is… well… He shouldn't be trying to use his dick without your permission, right?" There was a venomous look on the Asian doll's face. She had always been a little hostile to her new-found pet, knowing that Andrea preferred his mouth to hers. Andrea assumed what Kim was saying was just out of jealousy, but she did have a point.

Andrea looked at the strange toy again. She knew for a fact her desperate little fiancé jerked off unsupervised whenever he was home alone. It didn't really bother her, but maybe it should. It might be fun to have a little more control. Plus, the little plastic thing would look adorable on her man. Still, the whole thing seemed just a little too extreme.

She was about to laugh it off and put it back in the box. The idea of making her fiancé wear the adorable little chastity device seemed too dominatrix-like, and perhaps even cruel, but she was stopped by something another girl said.

Heather laughed. "He's not going to wear that, Kim." The slinky little redhead with oversized tits shifted enticingly in her skimpy sweat-shorts and undersized t shirt. She looked like she was wearing a hooters uniform, but this was her idea of casual. "No guy is going to let you lock his thing up like that."

Andrea stiffened. She felt suddenly, deeply offended. Her pet would do anything she wanted.

Kim just looked at Heather and smiled knowingly, as if she had personal experience that contradicted the younger redhead's statement.

Heather spoke again. "No guy is ever going to wear that." The young redhead seemed sure of her statement. She had barely started at the club, and had only ever known confident, big-dicked studs. She obviously couldn't even imagine that a whole other class of men existed. Of course, even if she did understand the malleability of sweet, nervous men, Andrea doubted the naïve little redhead could ever imagine the total subservient devotion of her pathetic little pet. She could sometimes barely believe it herself, but she had come to trust it.

Plus, Heather's words felt like a challenge, and Andrea was just drunk enough to never back down from a challenge.

Andrea picked up her cellphone and called Tim, who she had told to stay in the bedroom for the party. "Sweetie, come on out here. I've got something for you," she said giving Heather a wicked smile and a wink.

"I thought… you said not to…"

"I changed my mind," Andrea said. "I want to show off my sweet little pet."

The grown strippers all giggled like schoolgirls as they waited for Tim to arrive. It was only a minute before he stepped sheepishly into the room. It was most guys wildest fantasy to walk into a room like this, but Tim looked deliciously uncomfortable. He knew he didn't belong surrounded by this many beautiful women. His legs looked to be shaking underneath his soft, grey sweatpants.

"Come here," Andrea said reassuringly to her pet as he stepped nervously into the room. She pat her knee, as if lovingly coxing a dog forward. He walked into the room, eyes down, trying not to look at all the sexy girls. The girls all watched him, giggling to each other in deliciously naughty expectation.

When Tim finally reached her, standing in front of where she sat, his body swaying with nervous tension, she smiled sweetly at him.

"Pull down your pants," she said.

He inhaled deeply, his eyes going wide with absolute terror.

Andrea sighed. She took one look in those eyes and knew that no amount of loyalty or obedience was going to make this scared little man pull down his pants in front of all these beautiful women. So instead, she leaned forward and did it for him.

She grabbed his waistband with both hands, and with one quick jerk, she pulled down his sweats and underwear, dropping them to his ankles so he stood there in just a t shirt, his nervous dick shriveled even more than usual.

The room exploded in laughter. Heather covered her lush red lips to hide her laughter, eyes wide with shock and disbelief as she stared at Tim's shrunken prick. Tim closed his eyes, but took no action to retrieve his pants, or even cover himself. He stood there in humiliated shock, unable to move.

"Hey," Andrea purred sweetly to him, her voice cutting through the cackling laughter. "Hey. Look at me."

He opened his eyes, focusing on her and she smiled sweetly and reassuringly up at him. "I love you. And your adorable little dick looks especially cute tonight."

His eyes locked on her, focusing on her acceptance as the beautiful girls continued to laugh all around him, their beautiful voices musical and sensual, but their tone harsh and mocking.

Andrea gave him a little wink and said, "I got you something." She held the chastity device on the flat of her hand, holding it out like an offering.

"Wha... what is it?"

Did he already know? Was that recognition in his eyes? Was he just pretending? She studied him, trying to see if he was just playing, if secretly, he knew all about these kinds of toys.

"It's for locking your dick up," she finally purred. "So, it can't get hard, unless I allow it." She held it up to his body, holding it next to his shrunken penis. "I think it might be fun, and it's going to look so cute on you. Can I do it? Can I lock your little dick up?"

The girls all around them were still laughing at her adorable, ashamed little fiancé, and it made Andrea tingle. She was having fun. She had been letting him pretend that her utter ownership of him was a secret, but it felt so exciting to have it all out in the open now. From now on, her desperate little cuckold pet was going to have to get used to being paraded for her amusement.

"Lock it?" Tim swallowed. "How... For how long?"

"I haven't decided yet," Andrea purred, feeling deliciously nasty. It felt hot and electrifying to be displaying her power for all her friends to see. "It doesn't matter how long I lock it up for, though. I'm not really asking permission, Sweetie. It's actually an order. I am going to ask you again, and you're just going to be a doll, and say yes. Any other answer, besides yes, is going to make me very disappointed. Do you understand?"

Tim nodded, his body trembling.

Andrea rewarded her pet with a beautiful smile. "Now… Let me ask you sweetie: Can I lock your little dick up in this chastity thing? Can I seal it away so that you can't use it unless I say so? Can I lock it so it's painfully limp no matter how excited and needy my perverted little pet gets? Please? Pretty please?"

Tim made a tiny, almost invisible nod.

Andrea felt a rush of power, almost like a tiny orgasm moving through her body. She knew he'd say yes to anything she wanted, but part of her still couldn't believe he'd say yes to this. "'What? I can't hear you," she teased. "Tell me I can lock you up in my little cage for as long as I like. Tell me I own your dick."

Tim stared into her eyes, seeming to tune everything out but her; ignoring the cold room, the chastity cage, the coffee table covered in sex toys, and the room full of gorgeous strippers laughing at him; he only saw her as he spoke in a soft, but clear voice. "You can do anything you want to me. You can lock me up in your cage. You own my heart, and you own my dick."

Andrea clasped the chastity device over his dick. "That is so romantic," she purred.

The girls all exploded in laughter, but she meant it. She felt blissfully proud of her loving pet. She looked up at him, and he looked at her adoringly as she gently locked the padlock closed. She broke eye contact with Tim to glance at the redheaded young stripper who said it couldn't be done. She smiled triumphantly at Heather, and the slinky young girl stared back at her with awe.

Andrea looked back up at her pet, gave his naked ass a pat and said, "Okay. I'm done with you for now. Go back to the room."

He sheepishly pulled up his pants and walked out of the room, all the gorgeous strippers in the room laughing as they watched him slink away.

As it got later, the party started to change. Some girls left; the rest of the girls started drinking even more. Everyone was getting drunker, wilder and more loose. Many of the luscious strippers were making out with their girlfriends, or their friends-with-benefits, grinding against each other on the couches and chairs that filled the living room, none of them shy or embarrassed.

Andrea sat on a small loveseat between the gorgeous Asian Kim and the slinky redhead Heather. The three of them were all very drunk. Andrea wished she could send all the girls home. The drinks and the thrill of the chastity cage had her wet and craving Tim's tongue. Of course, most of the horny strippers in here didn't care who was watching, but she knew her shy little pet would be so much more comfortable servicing her in the peaceful quiet of their room. Still... She was craving him.

As if reading her thoughts, Kim leaned against her and purred in her ear. "Why don't you bring your fiancé back out here? Ask him how he likes being all locked up."

The Asian stripper's breathy whisper tickled Andrea's neck, giving her a flash of heat between her legs. This time she didn't bother with her cellphone. "Tim!" she called out through the house. "Come here, Pet!"

Tim hurried into the room, his eyes wide and his face beet-red when he saw all the beautiful girls making out around them. He stopped in front of the couch, where Andrea sat between the exotic Asian stripper and the luscious pale redhead. Kim was leaning close to Andrea, letting her hands rest on Andrea's curves, both girls bubbly with alcohol.

"How's the toy," Andrea said. "Does it hurt?"

"A little," Tim admitted.

Kim laughed viciously. "He'll get used to that," she said, giving Andrea's hip a squeeze and cuddling closer.

"Show us," Andrea said. "Drop em," she pointed at the ground by his feet.

Tim swallowed hard and forced a nervous smile, but this time he obeyed. He looked around, seeing no one else was really paying attention to him this time, and then he dropped his pants and underwear to his ankles. He stood there, skinny, nervous and pale, his shrunken dick pressed even smaller by the rubberized plastic cage.

Kim, Andrea and Heather all laughed.

"I still can't believe it," Heather said as she began to stand. "I'd love to stay and see what else you guys do to this poor guy, but my boyfriend is waiting out front."

Andrea and Kim both said goodbye, then Heather turned to Tim. She leaned slightly forward, her cleavage cast enticingly ahead as she purred to Tim softly, as if speaking to a pet. "You are a sweet little guy. Maybe some day, if I get bored of guys with big muscles and huge dicks, I'll find myself a nice little pet like you." She then pat him on the head and left.

Tim stood there swaying slightly, swallowing hard, obviously wavering between painful arousal and powerful humiliation.

Andrea watched her pet, feeling his aching need from four feet away. She pulled the Asian stripper closer, the electric excitement becoming unbearable. Kim took the squeeze as an invitation and turned, squirming against her, and kissed her on the lips. The Asian's big tits pressed against Andrea's smaller chest as the Asian purred. "Let's test it out. Make sure it works," Kim licked the side of Andrea's long thin neck with her wet, pink tongue. Kim's soft, skillful hands began to touch caress Andrea's ribcage and one of her breasts through the soft fabric of her t shirt.

Andrea shivered at the Asian stripper's touch. The woman's tongue and her soft hands felt good. It had been months since she'd let the slender brown girl with the massive fake tits, feather-soft skin and silky black hair go down on her, and although she preferred the well-trained tongue of her fiancé, the woman's touch still made her shiver and moan.

Andrea turned her face towards Kim, and they kissed again, the woman's tongue pushing aggressively between Andrea's lush, glossy lips. Kim threw one leg over Andrea's lap, and straddled her, taking hold of the sides of her face possessively as she continued her passionate kiss. Andrea shivered, her pussy beginning to flood with aching need. She looked across the Asian's face at her fiancé, as he stood quiet and helpless, pants around his ankles, pink cage locked on his soft little prick. Andrea looked up at the needy, desperate eyes of her fiancé. She could imagine how much that little dick of his wanted to swell, and she wondered if it hurt, pressing against the pink plastic of his little cock-cage. Instead of inspiring sympathy, the thought made her even more excited.

"Let's take this to my room," Andrea purred to Kim.

Kim slithered off her lap and held her hand as Andrea rose to her feet.

"Come along, Pet," Andrea commanded.

Tim followed behind the two gorgeous strippers, frantically pulling up his slacks as the girls swayed ahead of him, holding hands like schoolgirls.

Tim stood out of the way by the door as Andrea and her Asian stripper friend stood in front of the bed. They kissed a moment, and Kim began to take control, peeling Andrea's t shirt up over her head and throwing it aside. Andrea stood there, perky tits, nipples erect and pink, staring at the gorgeous Asian. Kim peeled off her own black sports-bra, releasing her majestic, artificial breasts. Andrea licked her lips. Those firm, round tits really were amazing to look at, standing tall and magnificent from the Asian's slinky brown frame. Kim kissed Andrea again, their naked breasts pressing together, nipple against nipple. Kim released her lush, Botox enhanced lips from Andrea's, a line of saliva still connecting their mouths, then the Asian pushed Andrea savagely back onto the bed. Andrea gasp at the sudden force, feeling the intense, powerful thrill of being treated like someone's toy. She lay at the edge of the bed, spike tipped heels still planted on the floor as Kim began squirming her slim frame between Andrea's long legs. The luscious Asian leaned over the slinky blonde and began kissing and sucking her way down Andrea's neck.

Andrea shivered with pleasure as the Asian stripper licked down her neck to her chest. The Asian's silky skin, and incredibly soft tits rubbed against Andrea's smooth flesh, making the slim blonde bite her trembling lip in growing anticipation. Kim kissed and sucked Andrea's tits as Andrea reached up and caressed the Asian's petal-soft skin. Across the room, Tim watched, his breathing hard and his dick painfully locked.

Kim had each of Andrea's ripe breasts in each of her hands, as she kissed lower, her lush lips leaving lipstick marks on Andrea's smooth brown skin. Tim stood watching, staring into Andrea's eyes as another woman began to peel off her skirt. Andrea lifted her ass off the bed, letting the Asian pull her skirt and panties off in one smooth action.

Andrea bit down harder on her lower lip, staring into her fiancé's eyes, as the Asian stripper's hands closed back over her Andrea's tits. Andrea let out a moan as Kim's red, Botox filled lips pressed against her soft, pink pussy-lips. The Asian's expert tongue began exploring Andrea's wet warmth, as her pet watched, desperate and helpless in his little pink cage.

Kim slurped between her thighs, licking inside her cunt one moment, then teasing her hard, sensitive clit the next.

Andrea had her hands in the Asian's silky black hair, caressing her as she began to writhe beneath her.

The situation and sensation were driving Andrea crazy, and she wished there was a big, hard cock available. She was so wet, and so hot, every touch thrilling and electrifying, she craved a huge, hot, throbbing cock inside her. "Oh fuck," she whimpered. "Oh fuck. I'm so wet. I'm so fucking horny."

Kim looked up from between her legs, face smeared with glistening juices, and she held up a toy. The devious Asian girl must have secretly snatched the huge dildo from her table of presents and been waiting for her chance to use it.

Andrea smiled glowingly at the black-haired beauty. "You are so bad," she said.

"I'm going to fuck you so good," Kim responded with her own, devious, glowing smile.

Andrea spread her legs wider and let her head fall back onto the mattress. Andrea took a deep, relaxing breath, then let it out with a soft, moaning whimper as the fat dildo began to push inside her dripping wet cunt. The exotic stripper kissed Andrea's inner thigh, beginning to ease the dildo back out of her, making her shudder with every rippled contour of the toy.

"Yes," Andrea moaned. She looked down at the dark-haired stripper, her natural, exotic beauty both highlighted and contrasted by her artificial, bimbo-like augmentations. Over the Asian's shoulder, she could see her fiancé, standing and watching helplessly. She smiled at her pet. "Drop your pants, sweetheart," she said. "I want to see your cute little cage."

He began to obey, as Kim smashed the dildo deep inside Andrea's hot, wet cunt once more. Andrea gasped with stunned pain and pleasure, then she laughed with delight, "mmmm, fuck, that's such a big, hard dick."

She stared into her pet's eyes as Kim began to drive the toy back and forth vigorously inside her. Tim stood with his pants around his ankles, his soft dick squished in the adorable pink cage. She moaned, her lips forming luscious shapes as the toy moved firmly and expertly in her soft, wet womb.

Kim purred in her delicious accent. "I love fucking you, Andy. I love your perfect pussy." She then bowed her head forward and began to gently suck Andrea's clit, while skillfully moving the dildo inside her. All the excitement of teasing and humiliating her fiancé suddenly paid off, and Andrea already began to shiver and shake with orgasm. She felt her muscles tense as a throbbing pulse echoed up her spine. She felt the rhythmic licks of Kim's wet tongue on her clit as the huge ridges of artificial cock slid across her sensitive, quivering flesh.

"Yes," Andrea whimpered. "I love getting fucked. You're so good. You're so fucking good, Kim. I love it. I love how you use that big, gorgeous toy dick. Fuck me. Fuck me, yes!"

She quivered from her toes to her eyelashes as the orgasm moved from her core to her extremities. Then, finally, the shaking passed, and she began to relax once more.

Kim pulled the dildo from inside her and bowed to her pussy, lapping at the warm juices that were flowing from inside her. "Yes," Andrea whimpered, looking at Tim, her hands on Kim's head. "Yes. Oh, fuck yes. That's so good. Oh fuck."

When Andrea totally relaxed with a deep shudder and a powerful sigh, Kim pulled her face from between the thin, brown thighs and looked up at the blonde. Kim saw Andrea staring lovingly at her fiancé, then looked back over her shoulder at him. Her face showed a momentary annoyance, then she shrugged.

"Come, little bitch," Kim said in her distinct accent. "Come give your fiancé a kiss. Tell her how lucky you are that she lets you watch her get pleasured by a woman you don't deserve to speak to."

Tim looked at Kim, then back at Andrea. Andrea smiled warmly and held out her arms for him. He rushed over, pants still around his ankles and snuggled on top of her. He lay on her, pants around his ankles, kissing her. "Thank you," he said breathlessly. "Thank you for letting me be here for that."

In spite of the physical intensity of the frustrated need throbbing through her fiancé, he showed no sign of being upset about being locked away in his little cage. Perhaps he understood what Andrea had just realized, that Kim would have never allowed him in the room for a show like that if his dick wasn't pressed into painful chastity. She kissed her pet on the lips, driving her tongue into his mouth. She reached down and squeezed his small, pale ass, pulling him close, feeling his rubber-coated plastic cage pressing down against her.

Andrea hugged her fiancé close, feeling his aching hunger pulsing against her satisfied body. She giggled at his tense desperation, running her fingernails across is back as if they were fucking, purring in his ear teasingly. She felt herself getting turned on all over again. She could feel the soft surface of his hard little cage, pressing against her wet, recently fucked pussy. It felt nice, and she worked her hips, rubbing herself against it, smothering him in slick wetness as she teased her own cunt with the rubberized plastic that was locked over his aching little prick.

She wrapped her legs around him, locking her ankles behind the small of his back and purring in his ear. "Fuck me," she purred. "Fuck me with your little toy."

He began to obey, wiggling his body against hers, grinding his cock-cage against her hot, wet cunt.

"Mmmmm," she purred. "Good boy. Good little bitch." She felt tingles of pleasure as the chastity device slid across her opening and pressed against her still engorged clit.

Behind them, Kim laughed maliciously. "Oh Andy, your little girlfriend actually is pretty cute. Do you want me to go ahead and fuck her too?"

Andrea looked at the gorgeous, buxom Asian, standing there with the massive dildo. The toy glistened with her own juices and the beautiful exotic looking stripper was smiling with excitement. Andrea had always thought the girl was purely a lesbian, but she was clearly thrilled at the idea of violating Andrea's fiancé with the realistic toy dick.

Tim had buried his face in the crook of her neck, his body trembling, either terrified of what the Asian stripper was offering to do to him, or terrified of showing Andrea how much he wanted it.

Andrea pet her little man's hair comfortingly. "Yes," she said. "Yes please. Fuck him. Fuck my fiancé with that big dildo. Fuck him right on top of me. It will be so romantic." She caressed Tim's back lovingly.

Kim smiled wickedly. "I wasn't planning on doing it romantically."

"It's okay," Andrea said. "I'll find it romantic. Besides, it won't be the first time my sissy's cunt has been used. He pretends not to, but I know he likes it rough." She squeezed her pet closer, feeling his soft skin and his thin frame pressing against her as she hugged him with both arms and legs. "Fuck him," she purred. "Fuck my little bitch just like he's your little bitch too."

The dildo was already slick with juices, but Kim added to it, spitting a huge mouth full of saliva onto the tip. Drool began to run down the thick, contoured shaft as Tim's body shivered with expectation.

Andrea purred in her fiancé's ear. "Mmmmm. I can't wait to feel you getting fucked on top of me. Your skin feels so nice. Your body feels so good. My sweet, gentle little bitch." She kissed his earlobe and let her tongue flick and tease him.

Kim leaned forward; her massive tits framed beautifully by her strong, slender arms as she pressed the tip of the toy to Tim's quivering little asshole. She held it there for just a moment, twisting it slightly to tease his hole, then she suddenly punched forward and pummeled the toy into him.

Tim let out a high, broken and feminine sounding whimper as his rectum was impaled with thick, artificial cock.

Kim laughed wickedly at Tim's weak, girly cry. Andrea laughed too. "Oh Sweetie, you sound adorable." She hugged him closer, kissing his cheek and purring into his ear.

Kim's face was lit up with thrilling excitement as she jerked the toy back and slammed it forward again mercilessly. As Tim's body was pummeled forward with another pathetic whimper, Tim's cock-cage ground against Andrea's clit making her shudder with thrilling sensation. "Yes," she moaned. "Fuck him. Fuck my little bitch."

Kim smashed the toy back and forth again, and again Tim whimpered deliciously, his chastity cage rubbing against Andrea's clit. She ran her nails across Tim's back, purring in his ear, staring up at the beautiful, but suddenly vicious looking Asian. Kim had an impassioned scowl on her exotic face as she hammered her toy back and forth in Tim's tight, aching asshole. Tim whimpered with each thrust, and Andrea moaned as the toy that locked his dick in limpness, rubbed against her hot, wet cunt.

Andrea worked her hips, grinding herself against her man's locked prick, smearing hot, wet juices all over his helplessly limp dick. She moaned as she heard him whimper, clawing his back as the Asian stripper fucked his tender asshole with the massive dildo. "Oh fuck," Andrea purred into his ear, her body sizzling with electricity. "I feel so close to you. I love feeling you like this. I love sharing this with you."

He whimpered and groaned, unable to articulate his feelings through the sensation of being hammered by the vicious Asian stripper. Andrea pressed her tongue into his ear, purring as she clawed him and Kim abused his rectum. Andrea purred and moaned, writhing against her fiancé with a steady rhythm, her soft, slender body shivering as she felt another orgasm building.

Andrea closed her eyes, tonguing Tim's ear, purring as the rhythm of their grinding bodies fell into pattern. She felt shivers of pleasure moving through her body as her fiancé continued to whimper with each thrust of Kim's toy. Andrea opened her eyes and looked at Kim. The beautiful Asian stripper had one hand down the front of her yoga pants, rubbing herself as she violently pounded Tim's rectum with the massive, artificial dick. The woman's silky black hair swayed across her skin and tickled her beautifully sculpted, artificial tits, which jiggled with every forceful thrust.

Tim's whimpers continued, but the quality of them had changed: less pleading and more surrender; less pain and more shivering, tingling pleasure. Andrea continued to lick his ear as she purred, "Good pet. Good little bitch. I love feeling you get fucked."

She watched the beautiful Asian, fingering herself as she brutally hammered her pet. She looked stunning and beautiful and absolutely cruel as Andrea tingled closer and closer to orgasm.

Andrea purred into her pet's ear. "I love feeling you get fucked. You're so good at getting fucked. A natural, little fuck-doll." Every movement of her fuck-doll's body made Andrea shiver with growing pleasure, as the chastity device rubbed back and forth across her tingling flesh.

Kim bit her lower lip, her whole body beginning to spasm as her fingers began to bring her to orgasm. The dark, luscious stripper jammed the dildo as deep as it would go in Tim's ass, then released her grip on it. She dropped to her knees behind them and bit Tim's ass. She chomped down hard enough to leave teeth marks on Tim's tender white ass-cheek.

Tim let out a high pitched "yip" sound then his body instantly went rigid with jerking orgasm. Hot sticky jizz leaked out from the gaps in his cock-cage and were smeared across Andrea's clit as she continued to grind against him.

"Yes," Andrea moaned. "Oh yes. My little bitch. My good little bitch." She too began to shudder as a second, softer but still thrilling orgasm pulsed through her. "Good boy. Good bitch. You're so sweet. Such a sweet, obedient fuck-doll. I love feeling you get fucked in the ass."

Tim went limp above her, his body drained from the intensity. He continued to hide his face in the crook of her neck, suddenly shy of the cruel Asian stripper behind them. Andrea caressed the back of his neck and his hair, purring, "My pet. My sweet little pet."

Kim moved on top of Tim's body; her massive tits mashed against his back. Andrea kissed the gorgeous Asian stripper over the shoulder of her spent, panting fiancé, both women's bodies hot and sweaty against his slim, bony frame.

Andrea smiled at her gorgeous friend. "Thanks for coming to my party," she said with a teasing smile.

"I enjoyed it," Kim purred. "We should do it again after the wedding. I can bring a girlfriend. We can make it a regular thing, like game-night, only it will be, abuse the little bitch night."

Andrea laughed. Petting the humiliated little bitch as she smiled at the exotic stripper. "He's feeling shy now, but considering the sticky mess he made all over me, I think he'll love it as much as I will."

Kim kissed her again and purred, "I don't care if he likes it. I'd rather have you all to myself, but it's okay. If I have to share...." She grabbed a fistful of Tim's hair and jerked his head back, so she could see his face, then she kissed him, pressing her tongue into his mouth. She kissed him for just a moment, then moved her mouth from his lips to his cheek, where she bit him savagely. "I can find ways to make it fun." She then released her grip on Tim's hair, kissed Andrea, once more, and slithered off their bodies.

As the stunning Asian stripper got dressed, Andrea hugged her fiancé close once more. Her body was warm with satisfaction and her heart warm with joy as she soothingly kissed his damaged cheek.

Tim whispered in her ear. "I can't wait till we're married, and I get to actually have sex with you."

Andrea smiled, caressing his soft skin, wondering to herself is she was actually going to keep her end of that deal. She lowered her foot and used her big toe to tease the base of the dildo that was still jammed inside him, making it wiggle, and laughing at the noises he made as it did.

BBC Wedding Night

"Do you, Andrea," the preacher's clear voice carried across the church, "Take this man to be your lawfully wedded husband, to love and to cherish, in sickness and health, good times and bad, for as long as you both shall live?" Andrea had, of course, had them remove any part of the vows that implied she couldn't be getting plowed whenever she wanted by bigger, better cocks, but she doubted anyone noticed. To all the people watching, she looked like a perfect, fairy-tale bride, in her long white gown, lace and satin everywhere. Her friends all knew the truth, of course. She loved to show off her power over her pet. And she loved flirting with other guys right in front of him, letting everyone know what a good, submissive little cuck her man was. But Tim's family had no idea. They didn't even know what she did for a living. She was always on her best behavior in front of them.

She looked at her little pet now. He looked clean and handsome in his tuxedo. No one would suspect he was wearing pink lace panties underneath his pleated black slacks. People seeing him now, would be surprised to see him with a girl as fit and gorgeous as her, but they wouldn't suspect him of being her desperate little bitch. She smiled at her cuckold. "I do," she said.

"Tim. Do you take Andrea to be your lawfully wedded wife. To love, cherish and obey, in sickness and in health, good times and bad, for as long as you both shall live?"

Andrea smiled under her white lace veil. She had told him he didn't have to include the obeying part. They both knew who was in charge, but he had insisted on having it in his vows. She realized now; she wouldn't have had it any other way.

"I do," Tim said.

The preacher spoke again. "I now pronounce you man and wife. Tim, you may kiss the bride."

Andrea moved closer as Tim nervously raised her veil. He pressed his lips to hers and she pushed her tongue into his mouth. Their tongues writhed together for a few moments then they parted, both smiling with joy. All the wedding guests began to cheer and applaud. Andrea pushed her cheek against Tim's and whispered in his ear, "I bet you tasted it. I just finished blowing my boss right before he walked me down the isle."

She moved back, smiled at him once more, then kissed him again, giving him another chance for a taste of the powerful seed whose musky flavor still danced across her tongue.

They then both turned to the crowd of their family and friends, as the preacher announced them to all as man and wife.

After the wedding reception, after all the dancing and drinking, Andrea and her new husband finally made it back to their newlywed suite. She still wore her storybook wedding gown, and he still wore his perfectly tailored tuxedo.

Back in the room, they started making out. They sat next to each other on the heart-shaped newlywed bed, touching and kissing each other frantically. Suddenly he stopped, breathless and dizzy with need, his desperate little erection throbbing in his slacks.

"Are we going to… we're married now… that mean's I get too…"

"Yes," she said, smiling warmly and caressing his cheek. "You get to have sex with me tonight. But not just yet. We have to take our time. I want to do this just right."

He nodded. Too excited to complain and ready to do anything she wanted to make things right.

"Good boy," she said. "We have a few minutes before my friend gets here…"

"Your friend?" Tim interrupted, excitement and disappointment both on his face.

"Didn't I mention. I made a new friend, and he's fucking amazing. And best of all, he has no problem letting my sweet little cuck watch him use his big, amazing cock on me. You can sit right there, at the edge of the bed, as he fucks me right in front of you. Doesn't that sound amazing?"

The erection, still throbbing in his slacks, told her it sounded amazing to him, but his nod of agreement showed hesitation.

"I told you," she promised. "You will get to have sex with me tonight. But I also told you I want it to be perfect. That means me getting hammered a big, hard cock first." She kissed his cheek, rubbed his back, and smiled wickedly at his expression. "Come on, Sweetie. Why don't you climb under this wedding dress and do what you do best till my lover arrives?"

Her needy pet's eyes instantly went to the way her dress flared out over her hips into a beautiful, wide train of silky skirts. He licked his lips and nodded, unable to resist the allure of her hot, wet cunt.

She lay onto her back and sighed with happiness, as her new husband slid onto the floor, crawled under her gown and began gently kissing the inside of one of her slender brown thighs. "Good pet," she purred.

She wore stockings and a garter, so instead of trying to stirp her panties, Tim kissed her wet cunt through the lace, then pulled them aside. He began to gently probe her hot pussy with his skilled tongue as she let her thighs rest on his shoulder, legs trailing down his back.

"Good pet," Andrea purred. "That's my good little cuckold hubby. A little softer… mmmm…. Yes Sweetie, get me ready to get fucked by a nice, big, black cock."

There was a moment of hesitation between her legs, then Tim began to lap at her with even more enthusiasm. Andrea laughed. "Mmmmm, I thought you might like that. And I'm going to love it. That big black cock is going to feel so good inside me, and you're going to love watching it. Right up close, front row seats, just like my little cucky pet deserves." She caressed her satiny dress, petting her new husband's head through the fabric. "Deeper," she said. "Mmmm. Good boy."

Andrea lost track of time, purring and softly moaning on the bed as her cuckold groom lapped and sucked at her hot, wet cunt underneath the gorgeous trains of her storybook wedding dress. But soon she looked up and saw the man she was waiting for. He had used the key she'd given him to enter the honeymoon suite. She had already fucked the man a dozen times, but the appearance of his powerful body and the mere thought of his amazing cock still made her cream with anticipation.

He was older, early forties, but built like a boxer. He stood well over six foot tall and had dark, ebony skin and striking green eyes. Andrea bit her lower lip at the sight of the powerful, older black man. She pushed her husband's head off her wet cunt and began to stand. Her husband, blocked by the fabric of the dress, didn't understand, and continued trying to lick her pussy and kiss her ass as she stood over him, dress covering him as he knelt on the floor. She walked towards her lover, letting the dress drag across her husband, till it finally pulled free and left him kneeling on the floor, looking after her, hair ruffled, tux wrinkled, and small erection clutched in his hand.

Andrea moved to the tall black man, wrapped her arms around his neck and began to kiss him passionately. Jamal's big, powerful hands moved up and down her pure white dress, caressing her slim torso through the lace and silk fabric. Their tongues dashed back and forth into each other's mouths, as Tim knelt staring in awe and her incredible beauty and her lover's incredible power.

Andrea broke off the kiss and stared into Jamal's eyes. "Thank you again for doing this, baby. I can't think of anyone I'd rather share me and my husband's special night with. I can't think of anyone I'd rather be the first one to fuck me right in front of my special little man."

Jamal laughed, giving her curved ass a squeeze through the lush fabric of the dress. "It's my pleasure," he said. "You are a sweet, sweet piece of ass. And I like being watched."

Andrea kissed Jamal again, purring and driving both hands down the front of his slacks. She began to caress his massive, soft cock. She licked his neck and kissed his chest, purring, "I apologize if he starts to cry when he sees how amazing your cock is."

Jamal laughed. "Wouldn't be the first time."

Andrea dropped to her knees, dress skirts flaring out across the floor, as she began to slide the huge, hardening meat out the top of her lover's slacks. She kissed the massive snake, feeling it harden in her hand and against the soft flesh of her plump red lips. She sat back on her heels, staring at the massive black cock, then she turned and looked at her new husband. She imagined she looked like some filthy wedding cake topper, elegant dress, virgin white with lace and satin, kneeling at the feet of a powerful black man with a huge, throbbing cock. She smiled at her new husband.

He wasn't crying. Tim was staring with frustrated awe at the massive black dong. His eyes were wide with wonder and fear as they saw the bulging veins that crossed the dark meat. Andrea stared at her pet as she leaned back in and gave the big black cock a lick from the base to the fat, purple tip. Jamal peeled off his shirt, revealing his chiseled torso as Andrea wrapped her lush red lips around his tip and began to slurp her way down his fat shaft.

She peeled down her lovers slacks the rest of the way, and then teased her fingertips along the tiny hairs on his strong, ebony legs. She opened her throat and took the massive girth and powerful heat of the black stud's beautiful cock down her esophagus. No longer looking back at her groom, she stared up at her lover, his meat buried down her throat. She hummed gently on him, as he affectionately caressed her carefully styled blonde locks.

"That's real nice, Baby," Jamal said in his deep, masculine voice. "That feels real, real good. But I didn't come here to get throated. I came here to fuck that hot, newlywed pussy of yours."

Andrea let the fat dick slip from between her lips. She held the saliva covered ebony cock, glistening in the lights of the honeymoon suite, gently stroking it. She looked back at her husband, kneeling on the floor behind her and she purred, "Sweetie, Come help me with this dress, please."

Tim scampered behind her. He kept his eyes down, afraid to look her lover in the face, but stealing peaks at his massive, glistening erection as Andrea gently stroked it, her new wedding ring sparkling. Tim began to work the laces on the back of her dress. Andrea looked back up at her lover, as Tim worked on her dress. She continued to stroke the big, black cock, leaning in to affectionately kiss and lick his powerful bullish balls.

Finally, Tim had loosened her dress and she rose to her feet. She shimmied out of the dress, letting it fall around her in a pile between her lover and her pet. Both men looked her up and down, eyeing her tight, curving little body in her silky bridal lingerie. Andrea held up her arms and turned so both their eyes could feast on her, then she stepped out of her dress and began strolling towards the bed. She moved slow and seductive, swaying like she was moving to the pole on a stage strewn with bills. Both men watched her, Jamal standing, his big black cock strong and impressively hard, Tim on his knees in his tux, cute erection poking out the zipper.

Andrea sat on the bed and smiled at Jamal. Jamal began walking towards her. His body was powerful and athletic. He didn't pay the slightest attention to her pet, kneeling on the floor, until he had almost passed him. Jamal suddenly gave Tim a gentle pat on the head with his massive, vein crossed, ebony hand. The gesture was almost indifferent, but confident and gentle, like a kennel master, casually acknowledging some puppy passing across his feet. It was just a single pat and then he moved on, but Andrea could see the warm glow of acceptance Tim felt at the gesture.

Andrea was dripping wet. She undid her garters and slipped off her panties, tossing them on the floor near her husband. "Fuck me," she purred to Jamal. "Come fuck my hot, wet, freshly married pussy with your big, beautiful cock."

Jamal was completely naked, his dark skin contrasting the bright colors of everything else in the room, his powerful muscles at ease but full of frightening potential as he strolled up to the bed. Andrea scooted back onto the heart-shaped newlywed-suite bed, still wearing most of her bridal lingerie as Jamal moved onto the mattress above her. Tim knelt on the floor between her discarded wedding dress and her discarded panties, erection in hand, staring with awe.

Andrea wondered if she should have put Tim in his little chastity cage for this, but then she decided: Let him cum if he wanted. She had promised him sex tonight, but if he couldn't wait for it, that was on him.

"Fuck me," she moaned to her gorgeous black lover as he moved over her, his ebony cock throbbing and glistening with saliva. "Fuck me while my husband kneels on the floor like a bitch, watching everything."

Jamal shut her up with a kiss, his big, powerful hands moving over her creamy tanned flesh, squeezing her curves and making her shudder with hungry need.

Tim wasn't stroking himself, just clinging to his small erection as he stared at the huge, muscular, black body hovering over his bride's slender frame.

"Fuck me," Andrea moaned between hot, wet kisses. "I want your big cock to be the first dick I get as a married wife."

Jamal spoke, his voice resonating power, but also a sense of patient kindness. "What about your little bitch, what does he want?"

"He wants it," Andrea moaned, her voice trembling with her own growing need, way past caring what her little pet wanted. "He wants it so bad."

"Tell me," Jamal said, turning his face a fraction and raising his voice. "Tell me you want me to fuck your pretty little bride."

Tim's nervous voice was almost a whisper. "I want it," he said.

"Beg me," Jamal ordered. "Beg me to fuck your hot new wife while you kneel on the floor and watch."

"Please," Tim said. "Please. I want you to fuck her. I want to watch so bad." Whether it was the excitement of the moment, or Tim finding comfort in being put in his rightful place, his voice was growing firmer and more resolved, his need and desperation less hidden. "I want to be here for this. I want to share this. I want to be part of her getting fucked by a real man, with a real cock."

Jamal laughed gently. "All right then. Go ahead and move closer. Don't be shy. Get your face right in there and have a good look."

Jamal then thrust forward, plunging his massive cock suddenly into Andrea's dripping wet cunt.

Andrea gasped as surprised pain and shocking pleasure shot through her core. "Oh fuck," she whimpered. "Oh fuck. That cock. That beautiful fucking cock. Oh, fuck yes."

Jamal held his fat BBC buried deep inside her, just letting it throb in her soft, wet womb, as Tim crawled carefully towards the bed.

Jamal let Andrea savor the depth of his meat, hot and hard inside her, then he began to slowly pull back, sliding every inch of his pulsating contours across her quivering flesh. She moaned deeply, then cried out in pain and ecstasy when he plunged himself inside her once more. "Oh fuck," she cried. "Oh, fuck yes. Your cock. Your big, gorgeous cock!"

Tim was at the edge of the bed now, looking up over the side, his head between both her and her lover's splayed-out ankles, watching like a puppy as Jamal slowly withdrew, then brutally rammed Andrea's cunt over and over in a torturously slow rhythm.

"Fuck me," she whimpered. "Oh fuck. I need it. I need your big cock."

Jamal grabbed a handful of Andrea's hair and tugged it firmly as if forcing her attention on his face. "You want it hard?" he asked. "You want your sweet, little bitch to see the woman he loves getting fucked like a dirty slut?"

"Yes," Andrea moaned. "I want him to see. I want him to know. Show my husband what a dirty, desperate slut I am for your big, amazing cock."

Jamal drew back suddenly, drawing his rock-hard erection out from inside her. "Turn over," he ordered Andrea. "Get on your hands and knees."

Andrea turned over onto her hands and knees. She raised her ass high and dropped her face to the mattress. She wiggled her ass towards Jamal's hot, black cock, begging to be fucked. She rested her face on one cheek, blonde hair sprayed out around her as she gazed back at her husband through her slender, spread thighs. He was staring with awe at her slinky body and her lover's massive, black cock.

Jamal rested a big, powerful hand on Andrea's small, curved ass and looked back at Tim. "Come on up here, little guy," Jamal said to her fiancé. "Get yourself a real good look."

As Tim began to nervously crawl onto the bed, Andrea purred happily. "Come on, pet. Get up here with me. Get under me. Let's sixty-nine while I'm getting smashed."

Tim crawled beneath her in the sixty-nine position, his head between her knees, and he instantly lifted his face and began to kiss her pussy and lovingly lick her clit. Andrea let her upper-body arch down onto her husband's frame. Her tits pressed against his tummy, her face on his hip, blonde hair draped over his erection as it jutted out of the zipper of his tuxedo. Her arms stretched out and she grabbed Tim's legs to stabilize herself for the vicious fucking she knew was about to begin. Andrea closed her eyes, enjoying the sensation of her groom lapping at her cunt, preparing herself for that big, black cock that was about to be inside her again. She shivered with anticipation, her hot, minty breath brushing across her husband's erection as he touched himself. "I'm ready," she told Jamal. "Fuck me. Fuck me hard. Fuck me on top of my husband on our wedding night."

Jamal rubbed his fat tip across the pink flesh of her opening, as Tim continued to lap devotedly at her clit. "You're his wife," Jamal said. "But you're my whore."

"Yes," Andrea moaned, her body aching with expectation. "I'm your whore. I'm your dirty, married whore."

With that, she gasped, feeling the powerful sensation of thick, hot meat being slammed against her cervix. Her body quivered and she moaned with deep, painful ecstasy as Jamal ground his meat deep inside her. He pulled back and plunged forward, ground deep insider her, then back and forward again. Tim's tongue still worked eagerly and obediently at her clit as the fat, powerful cock throbbed back and forth inside her. She whimpered and cried with each thrust, her body shuddering with intense sensation.

Her husband lapped at her cunt, his skilled tongue making her shiver as the enormous black dick filled her completely and repeatedly. She imagined her sweet pet's cute pale face beneath her, Jamal's thick, black balls dragging across it as that big cock moved back and forth. The image pushed Andrea over the edge, and she instantly began to explode with orgasm.

Her hot, moist moans of ecstasy passed across Tim's small erection as her body shivered with ecstasy. Her blonde hair tickled Tim's sensitive flesh as her body thrashed above him. Tim continued holding his dick, not stroking, as if trying to save himself for the promised intercourse, but precum dripped down his thin shaft and onto the pink panties he wore beneath his tuxedo.

Jamal kept pounding her cunt, even as her orgasm made her shiver and whine. Tim kept lapping at her pussy, slurping up her juices. More of her creamy juices were running down Jamal's rod to his fat, black balls, dripping down his balls and being smeared across Tim's face with every increasingly powerful thrust.

"Fuck!" Andrea cried out. "Oh fuck. Yes! It's so good. Your big, beautiful cock and my hubby's sweet little tongue. Oh yes! Oh, fuck yes!"

Jamal continued hammering her, as Tim continued eagerly massaging her hard clit with his soft tongue. Her orgasm grew and grew then it softened and dulled, but never stopped as she continued to be drilled deep and hard with hot, black meat. Tim's erection throbbed desperately inches from her face, but she ignored it, eyes closed, voice heavy with ecstasy, wet moans escaping her lush red lips.

"Fuck!" she moaned. "Oh fuck. I love it. I love your big, black cock."

Jamal moaned with pleasure. His thrusts smashed against her curved little ass, making her cheeks jiggle with the impact, and smashing her against her husband's face, pushing her entire body across her husband's frame as her ecstasy deepened and exploded into orgasm again.

Andrea lost count of her orgasms, as her cunt clung to the contours of fat cock, and her clit tingled against her husband's dedicated, little mouth.

Suddenly she felt an increased swelling in her lover's cock.

Jamal groaned with pleasure. "Yes. Oh fuck. Your tight married cunt feels so good. I'm going to cum. I'm going to cum so hard."

Andrea raised her head and looked back at Jamal over her shoulder. "Are you still going to do it?" she whimpered, unable to hide the desperate need in her voice. "Are you still going to do what I asked?"

Jamal laughed. "It's my pleasure," he said. He eased his cock back until it slid out of her. She almost pushed back against him, instinct still craving more of that big, black meat inside her, but she remembered her mission. She spun around, sitting on her husband's lap as she watched the ebony god stroking his rod over Tim's face. The fabric of Tim's tuxedo pants felt good against her wet, well-fucked cunt. She rubbed her clit, grinding against Tim's pelvis, his little erection bouncing against her ass. Tim's arms were under her legs, his hands reaching up to caress her ankles, fingers rubbing the silky sheen of her bridal stockings.

"Yes," Andrea whimpered. "Oh, fuck yes, Jamal. Do it. Oh fuck. Please do it."

Jamal was staring at her, her face and her tits and her long, slender body, still hugged by her slutty-looking bridal lingerie. Her blonde hair was drenched in sweat, her diamond wedding ring sparkling in the light as she played with her cunt. Jamal seemed to scan her up and down, taking all this in one more time, before he turned his attention down to her husband and began to cum all over his face.

She could see the surprise on Tim's face as the first wad of thick, hot cum shot across his cheek. The Andrea laughed happily, rubbing her clit as the next jet of sperm splattered across her husband's lips and nose. Tim had his eyes closed by the time the next squirt of potent seed splattered across his eyes, forehead and into his hair.

As always, Jamal came like a firehouse, drenching her obedient husband in more cum than the sweet little man had ever shot in his life. Andrea bit her lower lip, her fingers rubbing herself. She shivered, feeling the intense pulses of pleasure at seeing the powerful alpha male drench her sweet little man in his superior cum.

Jamal stroked out the last dribbles of cum, and they glistened on his fat purple tip. Andrea leaned forward and licked them off, then she leaned down and kissed her husband's sperm covered mouth. Her tongue, dripping with seed, slipped into her husband's mouth, but he didn't fight it. He kissed her back with eager abandon, his eyes squeezed shut and covered in spunk. Andrea licked his cheek, lapping up a mouthful of sperm, then purred in her husband's ear. "Now it's my turn to be the little cleanup bitch."

She began to lap at her husband's face, as she raised her body off his. She hovered over him, reaching down between them and grasping her husband's little dick. She purred in his ear as she lowered her body down, engulfing his thin erection in her hot, wet cunt.

Tim moaned in surprise and ecstasy as he finally experienced the wet heat of her pussy. Andrea began rocking against him, rubbing her clit once more as she affectionately licked another man's cum from his face. She was surprised, after all that fucking with superior cock, that she could feel Tim's little dick inside her. But it felt nice. It wasn't the same as being stuffed full of powerful, throbbing manhood, but Tim's dick touched somewhere different inside her, and it felt good.

Her body writhed against her husband, the lace covering her tits rubbing against the silk shirt covering his chest as she licked another man's cum from his jawline. Tim's hands moved across her back, squeezing her close as he whimpered with long denied pleasure. Andrea was surprised at how good it felt, fucking her husband. His sweet touch, his hard little dick pressing in just the right spot. She purred in his ear, licking more cum from his cheek and his hair.

Andrea whimpered, rubbing herself on Tim's cock, little shivers moving through her slim, perfectly tan body. Her bridal lingerie, all silk and lace, slid easily across her husband's tuxedo. Her cunt, still aching from the deep fucking she'd just gotten, tingled where her husband's dick massaged her. Tim was groaning in bliss, hugging her close to him, his face buried in the curve of her neck as she licked up morsels of another man's cum from his adorable face.

"I love you," she purred in his ear. "I love my obedient little bitch husband."

Tim groaned at her words, and the feel of her voice purring across his ear. He cried out as he began to explode inside her, and the feeling of that release, along with the intense closeness of Tim's body, also sent Andrea over the edge.

The two rocked against each other, orgasming in unison as the massively built black man they'd just shared their wedding night with, began casually getting dressed.

As they both panted with the aftershocks of orgasm, they began to kiss passionately.

"I love you," Tim moaned.

Andrea laughed and kissed him. "I love you too, Pet," she purred.

Tim was still a little breathless as he said, "You've made me the luckiest little bitch in the world."

Andrea laughed and then bit Tim's cheek affectionately. "My bitch," she said.

"Your bitch, forever," Tim agreed.

"Good boy," Andrea giggled, wiggling her body against her pet then finally sliding off his soft, little dick. "Wait here. I want to try and suck Jamal off one more time before he goes."

Tim smiled, giving his wife an affectionate pat on her perfect little ass. "Good luck," he said.

Andrea kissed his forehead and gave his hair a little ruffle before hurrying into the next room to properly thank the hot, black stud for her perfect wedding night.

The End

* 9 7 9 8 4 4 1 0 5 8 5 3 7 *